"Adelaide."

Her eyes flicked open

"Make them stop, Royce."

"What, Adelaide? What do you want me to stop?"

She didn't answer as he stroked the nape of her neck, feeling her go pliant in his arms. Streams of heat entered his body and burned in his veins. There it was again, that inexplicable hypnotic edge of desire present every time he touched her.

"You've got to tell me if you want my help."

"It's here." She motioned to the drawings on the floor with a slight tilt of her head. "They wake me up from a dead sleep and I'm compelled to come down here and draw these…these…"

"Pictures?"

"Yes."

His mouth went dry and he released her to pick up the nearest one, trying to conceal the creeping layer of revulsion the sadistic image churned in his gut.

"I don't know where they're coming from." She turned misty green eyes on him and he couldn't resist.

He reached out for her and pulled her against him, feeling the silkiness of her skin under his fingers. Smelling the sweet spicy scent of her hair. He closed his eyes for an instant to absorb the sensations, but the only thing he saw was the image of a c

JAN HAMBRIGHT

KEEPING WATCH

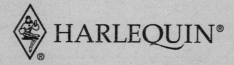

TORONTO • NEW YORK • LONDON
AMSTERDAM • PARIS • SYDNEY • HAMBURG
STOCKHOLM • ATHENS • TOKYO • MILAN • MADRID
PRAGUE • WARSAW • BUDAPEST • AUCKLAND

To the Protectors out there
who stand in the gap every day. Thank you.
To my husband,
who patiently puts up with Jan-on-deadline. I love you.
To my wonderful editor, Allison,
who liked this idea enough to buy it.
Thank you.

ISBN-13: 978-0-373-69486-0

KEEPING WATCH

Copyright © 2010 by M. Jan Hambright

Recycling programs
for this product may
not exist in your area.

Printed in U.S.A.

ABOUT THE AUTHOR

Jan Hambright penned her first novel at seventeen, but claims it was pure rubbish. However, it did open the door on her love for storytelling. Born in Idaho, she resides there with her husband, three of their five children, a three-legged watchdog and a spoiled horse named Texas, who always has time to listen to her next story idea while they gallop along.

A self-described adrenaline junkie, Jan spent ten years as a volunteer EMT in rural Idaho, and jumped out of an airplane at ten thousand feet attached to a man with a parachute, just to celebrate turning forty. Now she hopes to make your adrenaline level rise along with that of her danger-seeking characters. She would like to hear from her readers and hopes you enjoy the story world she has created for you. Jan can be reached at P.O. Box 2537, McCall, Idaho 83638.

Books by Jan Hambright

CAST OF CHARACTERS

Royce Beckett—He's the New Orleans detective assigned to protect the police department's beautiful sketch artist, Adelaide Charboneau, after an attempted abduction.

Adelaide Charboneau—She uses her unique abilities to expose evil by sketching composites of criminals for the NOPD. Can she and Royce find answers in time to save her from the fate in her own drawing?

Detective Hicks—He's the lead investigator in the case, and one of the good guys. Isn't he?

Chief Danbury—He comes off as a hard-nosed cop, but at heart he's a true believer in Adelaide's abilities, because she produces results.

Officer Brooks—He's bucking for a promotion, but is he willing to do almost anything to get it?

Professor Charles Bessette—He helped Adelaide understand her gift.

Miss Marie—She's the owner of Spells-4-U, Voodoo and More, but will Adelaide and Royce heed her warning?

Vincent Getty—He's bad all over.

Kimberly Beckett—She was abducted as a child. Now she's a grown woman with the mind of a five-year-old. Could the images locked inside her head help her brother, Royce, find the truth?

Chapter One

A brilliant flash of lightning jolted Adelaide Charboneau awake from a dead sleep.

She rolled over and stared up at the ceiling, praying this wasn't the beginning of another bout of insomnia, leading to a late-night drawing session in her art studio downstairs.

Thunder rumbled close by and vibrated the house, but her attention focused on the mini-blind as it clanked against the open window frame.

A storm was coming. She could smell it on the air slicing through the two-inch crack at the bottom of the sill. A storm and something more. Something she couldn't quite grasp.

Chills skimmed her bare skin and prickled the hairs at her nape.

She pulled back the covers, climbed out of bed and walked to the window, determined to shut out the uneasy sensation clawing through her, right along with the torrent of rain she knew was coming.

It was hurricane season on the Gulf Coast. An edgy time for the residents of New Orleans who instinctively turned their attention to the southern horizon, and their TVs to the weather channel.

She brushed aside the billowing sheers, pulled up the blind and locked it in place.

The sky lit up again, casting a white-hot glow like a net directly overhead.

Her focus riveted on movement in a cluster of azaleas near the gazebo.

The flash fizzled, but the image was burned on her brain. There was a man standing in her backyard.

Shaken, she closed the window, locked it and stepped back, trying to pick him out in the gloom as her eyes adjusted. Follow-up thunder rumbled, its vibration churning up fear in her mind. What was he doing here?

The answer came crashing into her consciousness with an explosion of shattering glass from somewhere in the massive house.

The back door? He was breaking in.

She stumbled forward, rushed the bedroom door, shoved it closed and locked it.

Adrenaline pulsed in her veins, putting her senses in a state of hyperalert. Was he already inside? Making his way through her kitchen and up the stairs? Had he seen her standing in the window?

The air was still, save the beginning tap of rain on the roof overhead.

Footsteps? She heard footsteps on the stair treads.

Determination pushed her to action. She wheeled around, looking for anything she could use to defend herself. Her gaze locked on a heavy candlestick perched on the corner of the dresser. She snatched it, sending the pillar candle crashing to the floor with a thud.

Grabbing her cell phone from the nightstand, she hurried to the closet, opened the door and crept inside, careful to pull it closed without a sound.

Shoving through the clothing, she pressed into the corner, turned her back to the wall and went to her knees.

Her hand shook as she opened her cell phone and dialed 911.

"Enhanced 911, what is your emergency?"

"A man just broke into my house through the back door." Her voice sounded muffled in the confines of the closet, but too loud in her own ears. "I think he's inside my house."

"Are you Adelaide Charboneau, 1532 St. Charles Street?"

"Yes."

"Stay on the line with me, Adelaide. I'll dispatch an officer to your location."

Squeezing the candlestick in her hand, she strained to hear his footsteps over the hammering rain.

"Please hurry," she whispered, feeling the walls of the closet protecting and smothering her at the same time.

She closed her eyes, trying to keep her fear in check. Help was on the way. Someone would come.

The familiar groan of the floorboards outside her bedroom door intruded into the white noise around her.

Her eyes flicked open in the dark. Her mouth went dry.

It wouldn't take him long to find her, pry her from her hiding place and—

The last graphic thought in her head evaporated with the sound of splintering wood. The bedroom door slammed against the wall.

He was coming for her.

DETECTIVE ROYCE BECKETT turned the windshield wipers on high and squinted to see the road in front of him through the frantic flap of the blades.

It was a torrential downpour, the sort he liked to watch from a well-worn chair, holding a bottle of imported beer. But not tonight, not in the middle of the personnel shortage plaguing the NOPD like a bad case of the flu.

The light at the corner of Canal and St. Charles Street turned red. He braked to a stop at the same time the portable police radio attached to his belt broke squelch.

He listened for the verbal traffic to follow, not that it

mattered; he was off duty for the night, headed home to get some z's.

"All units in the vicinity of St. Charles Street, please respond to a break-in in progress. 1532 St. Charles, the Adelaide Charboneau residence. She reports point of entry is the back door of the residence. The intruder is inside. I repeat, the intruder is inside. Use extreme caution."

Royce mouthed the name. Adelaide Charboneau. He'd heard it somewhere, but he couldn't place it.

Yanking the radio off his belt, he pressed the call button. "Detective unit thirty-four. I'm three blocks from that location. I'll respond. Send a backup unit."

"Copy unit thirty-four. Units forty-eight and thirty-two will be en route."

"Unit thirty-four clear."

Royce flipped on the lights, stomped on the gas pedal and shot around the corner onto St. Charles.

Home invasions were dangerous. Unpredictable. They could ignite faster than gas and a match.

He glanced at the house numbers every time the wipers cleared the windshield, but he didn't have to look very hard to see a man dragging a woman across the front lawn at 1532 St. Charles Street.

Adelaide Charboneau.

Jerking the steering wheel hard to the right, he slammed on the brakes and flooded the duo in the car's headlights. He unholstered his Glock 9mm, flung open the door and climbed out, using it for cover, as he leveled his weapon on the man holding a scantily dressed woman around the waist. Her feet dangled just above the ground, and she continually rammed her heels into the shin of his right leg.

"Police! Let her go!" he yelled, noting the man's description, and the ball cap obscuring his features. He didn't appear to have a weapon, but it was the one he couldn't see that was the most deadly.

Royce stepped out from behind the door, taking a couple of aggressive steps forward. "Let her go!"

The man staggered to a stop and turned to face him.

Royce held his breath. The moment of truth. The instant fight-or-flight decisions were cast and irreversible.

The suspect shifted his stance, lowered Adelaide onto the grass in front of him and locked her in a choke hold.

Caution worked through his veins. She was on the verge of becoming a casualty if he didn't do something.

Royce took another step forward. "Don't be stupid. Let her go." He closed the distance. Close enough to see the blindfold that covered her eyes and the duct tape wrapped around her wrists.

He went cold all over. This was an abduction? It had to stop here, but if he fired his weapon, he ran the risk of hitting her.

Tension cranked every muscle in his body into overdrive as he prepared to charge in for the takedown.

The suspect shuffled backward, dragging Adelaide with him to the edge of the yard and a thick cluster of azalea bushes.

He shoved her hard in Royce's direction and bolted for cover, leaving Royce without a clear shot.

The woman lurched forward, twisted her ankle and crumpled to the ground on her knees. Reaching up, she pulled the blindfold down and stared at him as he rushed toward her.

Royce kept his weapon trained in the direction the subject had taken, listening to the sound of heavy footfalls trailing the suspect's getaway through the bushes and into the alley.

He was soaked to the bone now. Rivulets of rainwater seeping under his shirt collar and rolling down his back. Sliding to a stop in the wet grass beside her, he glanced up to make sure the subject wasn't mounting a counter attack.

A squad car ground to a stop at the curb and cut its siren. Two officers jumped from the car and drew their weapons.

Royce pointed in the direction the thug had taken, and knelt next to Adelaide Charboneau.

"Are you okay?" he asked, swallowing hard as his gaze traveled the length of the flimsy pink nightgown she wore. It was soaked and sealed to her skin, clinging to her breasts, and leaving little of her body that wasn't accessible to his view.

Uncomfortable with the instant blaze of heat in his blood, he stood up and slogged out of his jacket. Bending down, he draped it over her shoulders. "Sorry it's wet."

She raised her face to his. "It's cover. Thank you."

A trickle of blood trailed from a small cut on her lip.

Concern jolted him, and he knelt back down on the grass next to her. "Your lip is bleeding. Did he hurt you?"

Adelaide ran her tongue over the tiny, insignificant cut on her lip. She'd probably gotten it when she tried to bite him. "It's minor, but I did twist my ankle when he pushed me, and I'm fairly shaken up."

"You put up a heck of a fight."

She nodded, realizing how cold she was even though the rain was tepid and the air warm. A shudder racked her body, followed by another, as she made an unsuccessful attempt to brush the wet hair off her face with the back of her bound hands.

"Can you get this tape off me?" She turned the plea on him, but she already knew the answer.

Reaching out, he stroked the hair back with his fingertips. "It's evidence. You'll have to wear it until the CSI team can collect it, but I can get you out of the rain."

Grateful, she touched his forearm with her hands. A wave of relief flooded her body. Help had come. It had come in the form of a man who for some overwhelming reason made her feel safe for the first time in weeks.

"I'm Detective Royce Beckett."

"Adelaide Charboneau," she whispered as he gently brought

her up onto her bare feet, as if she were made of something fragile. He put his arm around her shoulders and pulled her against him.

Heat ignited in her body, chasing away the chill. She swallowed hard, knowing if it weren't for Detective Royce Beckett, she'd be trying to kick her way out of a car trunk right now.

She pushed the haunting image into the back of her mind, knowing it would resurface, but not tonight. Tonight she was safe and she had every intention of relishing it.

Royce spotted a cluster of chairs on the veranda next to the open front door and aimed for them, but the moment he stepped forward, Adelaide let out a yelp of pain and sagged against him.

Without hesitation he scooped her up in his arms and carried her across the expanse of grass, up the steps and onto the porch. He carefully set her down on a wicker settee and stepped back.

In the glare and shadows of the headlights, he could see the intense shade of purple forming along the narrow shaft of her bare ankle. "You need to have that looked at. It could be broken."

For the first time tonight he finally got a solid look at her face. It was a fresh face, a beautiful face, he decided as she stared up at him with eyes the color of smooth jade.

The drone of another squad car hummed from up the block, and it pulled in just as the other officers appeared from around the side of the house using their flashlights to comb the darkness.

"Anything?" he asked, dragging his gaze away from Adelaide.

"Nothing. We saw a car pull away from the curb a block over, but we weren't close enough to get a description."

"Do an inside sweep in case the unsub had a partner. I'll call in CSI."

The two officers climbed the steps, drew their weapons and disappeared inside the front door.

Royce pulled the radio from his belt and called in the team, hoping the thug had left evidence he could use to nail him.

Two more uniforms sloshed up the walkway and stopped at the bottom of the steps.

"Miss Charboneau?"

Royce turned just as one of the officers took the stairs a couple at a time and knelt next to the settee.

A jolt of protectiveness jumbled his thoughts, and he had to fight the urge to step closer to her, to pull his jacket tighter around her shoulders, to cover the smooth expanse of her bare leg stretched out on the settee.

"Officer Brooks. It's a horrible night to be out." She gave a tired smile.

Brooks's face was stern as he stared at the tape locking her wrists together, then back up at her face.

"What happened?"

"A man broke into my house and tried to take me."

"Do you know who he is?"

"No, I never saw his face."

"You mean you didn't recognize him?"

"I mean I never saw his face. He blindfolded me in the closet."

"Dammit." Officer Brooks came to his feet and turned to face Royce. "She's the best sketch artist the department has ever hired. If she'd seen the bastard, she could draw him, and I'd catch him."

It hit him then, like a Mack truck on the 10 freeway. Adelaide Charboneau, NOPD sketch artist. In fact he'd just used a composite she'd drawn to catch a serial rapist. "I got a look at him."

Adelaide glanced up a him. "If you saw him, I can create a composite."

Royce pulled the image in his brain, then realized how

obscured the details were by the man's ball cap. "We'll give it a try, but between his hat, bad lighting and the rain, I'm not sure it'll make a difference."

A look of acceptance passed across her features, and she nodded in agreement. A gesture that seemed to him to be out of place in the exchange.

Glancing up, he watched a long white van pull up to join the string of cop cars bedazzled with flashing lights.

The whole neighborhood was awake now. People rubbernecked from their porches, dressed in their jammies. Fortunately the rain was letting up one bucket at a time, and dawn was just over the eastern horizon.

"It's clear, Detective." One of the uniformed officers stepped through the doorway, while the other one flipped on the porch light from inside the foyer.

"There are a dozen muddy footprints coming in across the kitchen floor, and broken glass at the point of entry. We'll take a look around the perimeter and turn it over to forensics."

"Thanks." Royce turned his attention back to Adelaide, noticing a shiver quake her body. He needed to get her inside and dried off.

Officer Brooks's radio broke squelch and Royce was relieved when his unit was called out by dispatch on an MVA.

"Take care, Miss Charboneau."

"I will." Adelaide raised her bound hands in an awkward wave and watched the two cops hurry for their car, nearly colliding with a woman carrying a case almost as big as she was.

She rushed up the steps, put the case down and shook off the rain before wiping a hand across her face and looking up at Detective Beckett.

"I'll be glad when hurricane season is over."

"How are you, Gina?" Royce stepped forward.

"Soggy." She reached into her jacket pocket and pulled out

a pair of latex gloves. "But I suspect you knew that, Beckett. Looks like everyone gets wet tonight. Let's just hope it doesn't flush all the evidence down the storm drain." She gloved up and looked at him. "It's your crime scene, what've ya got?"

"A break-in using the back door of the home. The unidentified subject crossed through the kitchen. Officer Jones indicated there are muddy tracks leading from the point of entry. The subject then attacked the occupant of the home, Miss Charboneau, and dragged her outside via the front door, then onto the lawn, where I confronted him."

Gina glanced over at Adelaide. "Glad you're okay, miss."

"Thank you."

"First order of business is removing the tape he used to bind her hands."

"Let's get her inside, then." Gina picked up her forensic kit and stepped inside the house.

"Can you stand?" Royce asked, glancing down at her swollen ankle.

"Maybe." She rocked forward and slid her legs off the settee, then put her bare feet on the floor.

Royce moved in next to her and helped her up. She put pressure on it, and recoiled when searing pain shot up her leg. She lifted her foot, only to have Royce catch her before she went down.

"No way. There's no way I can put full weight on it."

In one fluid motion he scooped her up into his arms again.

Embarrassment flooded her body and morphed on her cheeks in hot patches she could feel. The close contact jumbled her nerves and tensed her muscles, sending her body into another fit of shivering. She'd always wanted to be carried over the threshold, but this wasn't exactly what she'd had in mind.

"Try to relax," he whispered over the top of her head. "I'll get you warmed up in a minute."

That was as futile as asking the rain to stop in an instant. She sucked in a deep breath, willing the shaking to cease, but everything about the night conspired against her. She turned her face into his chest and closed her eyes.

Royce stepped in the front door, worried about the woman in his arms. Was she in shock? He couldn't blame her if she was. She'd been through a lot tonight.

He spotted Gina to the right of the foyer, motioning him to the sofa in front of a massive fireplace. Turning her back to them, she flipped the switch on the wall next to the mantel and flames ignited in the hearth, sending a wave of heat out into the room.

Royce carefully put Adelaide down on the sofa and stepped back. "She's freezing. Can you tack it up?"

"Yeah." Gina was already pulling the digital camera out of her kit.

"The blindfold, too. She was wearing it when I stopped the unsub outside." Royce stared at the soaked piece of cloth draped around her throat. "It looks like a kitchen towel."

"He must have improvised and grabbed it on his way through the kitchen." Gina raised her camera. "This won't take long, miss."

"Towels?" he asked.

"The linen closet in the upstairs hallway."

Gina squeezed off a shot of Adelaide's bound hands, and repositioned from another angle.

Royce stepped out of the parlor and glanced up the expansive staircase to the second floor. Moving forward, he turned on the light switch, firing up a massive chandelier suspended from the open foyer ceiling. The place smacked of money and elegance. Neither one a bad thing. Big bucks. Was it possible the subject had planned to kidnap Adelaide Charboneau and hold her for ransom?

Worry sliced through him, drawing him up the stairs to

the second-floor landing where the intensity of her struggle against her captor was apparent.

A vase lay smashed on the hardwood floor, swept from a low mahogany table. A large painting was cocked at an awkward angle above it. All the doors in the hallway were closed save one. Royce slowed his steps, careful to survey the damage for clues.

He clamped his teeth together when he reached the open door at the end of the corridor. The splintered wood at the kick plate indicated it had been kicked open. Anger jolted him, and he sympathized with the terror she must have experienced, hearing the intruder, knowing he was in her room.

Seeds of an old memory sprouted in his mind, but he quickly stunted them. The past was just that, the past.

Reaching around the jamb, he flipped on the light and stepped into the room. The closet door was open. A trail of clothing and broken hangers lay on the floor in front of it. She must have hidden inside, but the assailant found her.

Royce examined the layout of the bedroom, his gaze pausing on the massive bed against the south wall, at the bunching of covers thrown back. What had gotten her out of bed and into the closet? Taking one last look, he left the room and found the linen cupboard.

He pulled a couple of towels out and went back down to the parlor, where Gina was putting the coil of duct tape into a paper bag.

"What woke you up tonight?" he asked, coming around the sofa to hand her a towel.

"Wait," Gina said, just as Adelaide shook the towel open. "I've got to have the blindfold, too."

"Sorry." Adelaide waited as she cut the towel off and put it into a bag.

"The lightning. A flash woke me up, and I'd left the window open a crack. The blind was hitting against the frame and I got up to close it. That's when I saw him standing in my backyard."

"And you called 911?"

"No. Not until I heard him break a window in the back door of the kitchen."

"You hid in the closet?"

Fear hissed through Adelaide's body as the memory reconstituted in her mind. "Yes. That's when I dialed 911 from my cell."

"What happened next?"

She clutched the towel, pulling it up around her neck, trying to combat the surge of anxiety sliding along her spine.

"He kicked in my bedroom door and came into the closet after me."

"Did you get a look at his face?"

"No. I never saw him. He grabbed me, covered my eyes, taped my hands and—"

Reaching up, she milked a section of her hair to confirm a weird suspicion. "He clipped off a piece of my hair."

"Why would he do that?"

"I don't know, Detective. Maybe it's some sort of trophy to appease a fetish." Her voice threatened to give out, but she cleared her throat. "He was so strong, I couldn't get away."

Royce moved in next to her and sat down. "You fought hard. It wasn't your fault."

His words calmed the what-if game raging inside her head. What if she'd have called the police last week after she suspected someone had been in her house. What if she'd have put in a security system.

"Miss Charboneau…Adelaide?"

She glanced over at the detective, suddenly aware he'd spoken her name more than once.

"I'm sorry. It's just that…I think someone may have been in my house last week. I wish I could be one hundred percent certain, but I'm not."

Royce sat forward, letting his instincts take over. "How so?"

"I ran to Delesandro's Bakery to pick up my mother's birthday cake before two when they close, but halfway there I realized I'd forgotten my cell phone in my studio, and I was waiting on an important call. When I ran back into the house to grab it, there was an unfamiliar scent inside, and some of the work in my studio wasn't where I remember leaving it. It was like someone had shuffled through everything."

"Are you sure?"

"Yes. I always put my sketches away in a portfolio, but I found them scattered on the table. I suppose I could have forgotten, but I'm pretty consistent."

A tingle of caution crept along Royce's spine. Had the unsub cased her home for its layout before tonight? Judging by his violent entry, he knew exactly where to find her.

He watched her towel her hair, letting his gaze slide over her slender body no longer covered by his jacket. Hard to imagine she'd ever have been able to overpower her attacker. Maybe it was better that she hadn't. He might have really injured her. But he deemed her a fighter, judging by the mess upstairs, and her physical injuries. Still, the need to protect her welled inside him, festering and flooding into his brain like a drug.

"Would you like me to call an ambulance? You should have your ankle looked at."

"I'm going to ice it and call my mother. She'll take me in."

He nodded, noting the pink in her cheeks matched the color of her drying nightgown. He tamped down a flare of heat the observation fired in his blood and stood up just as one of the uniformed officers stepped into the foyer.

"Detective Beckett. There's something you need to see."

"Where?"

"Under the window on the back left side of the house."

"What room is that?" he asked Adelaide.

"It's my art studio and office." Her brows pulled together. "That's where I found my sketches out of place last week."

Royce moved for the front door, taking the flashlight the uniform handed him as he moved past. He stepped out onto the veranda, noting that the rain had stopped, and dawn was beginning to overtake the darkness.

He turned on the flashlight and took the steps quickly. Hanging a right, he walked around the right front corner of the house, spotting an officer with his light trained just below the windowsill.

"You got something?"

"Yeah. It's suspect, anyway. Sort of weird."

Royce stepped in next to the officer and aimed the flashlight beam on the same spot.

"What does it mean?" Officer Jones asked.

"I don't know."

The letters were scratched…no, carved into the siding of the house. It wasn't weathered. It looked fresh.

BEHOLD…and the beginning of another letter. "Is that part of an *E* maybe?"

"Could be." Royce slid the flashlight's beam down the siding and onto the soft earth, where a partial shoe print was pressed into the mud.

"Get Gina on this, see if we can match it to the tracks in the kitchen."

"Do you think they were made by the same person?"

Royce pondered the officer's question, but he didn't have an answer.

"We'll have to wait for a comparison." But there was one thing he knew for certain.

Adelaide Charboneau was in real danger.

Chapter Two

Royce paced in front of the chief's office door.

It had been two days since Adelaide Charboneau's attack, two days too many as far as he was concerned. Hell, he'd have put half the department shoulder to shoulder around her house if he could have.

"Beckett. Stop it, and get in here."

Relief would have been his response had Chief Danbury's voice not held its note of irritation for more than two beats.

He avoided the chair directly in front of the desk and chose to stand. "You heard about Miss Charboneau's attempted kidnapping?"

"Is that what it is now?"

"Her attacker blindfolded her and restrained her with duct tape. He was dragging her across the lawn when I got to the scene. We have to assume he planned to take her if I hadn't intervened. For what purpose, we don't know."

Danbury grunted, motioned to the chair and rocked back in his own.

A sit-down was a good indication he'd at least hear him out, up until the word "stake-out" came up, anyway.

"I've read the report, Beckett, and you know where we stand on manpower. I'm up to my armpits in shortfalls. The mayor is having a hissy fit because the knucklehead who snatched his mother's purse hasn't been apprehended yet.

Three cruisers in the motor pool have been vandalized in the last week, and this department is stretched as thin as my momma's gray hair."

"She's one of our own, Chief." If his statement registered with Danbury, it was in the way his eyes narrowed for an instant and his shoulders sagged.

"Spill it."

Royce sat forward, feeling tension crank the muscles between his shoulder blades. "I know this guy is coming back for her. I don't know when, I don't know why, I don't know how, I just know he is."

"Cut the drama, Beckett. How much time?"

"Three days, more if necessary."

Chief Danbury let out a puff of air and eyeballed him with skepticism from across the desk. "The report says the word *behold* was carved in the wood under a window. Any idea what it means?"

"No."

"Did you ask Miss Charboneau?"

"I didn't get the chance—"

"Then you better get cracking. You've got three days."

Had he heard correctly? Three days to prove a theory that had churned up from somewhere in his gut?

"Thanks, Chief." He stood up and hustled for the door.

"Don't thank me yet. If anything comes in, I'm pulling you off this."

He nodded and didn't turn around. He couldn't risk giving Danbury a chance to renege. It was going to be tough enough to hope another case didn't come in and push hers down on the priority list.

Hanging a left at the end of the hall, Royce headed for Gina's office, almost running into her as she stepped through the doorway.

"Hey, Ice Man, you better pull your head out of the clouds before you get hurt."

Royce stopped short and glanced up, irritated with himself for not paying attention. "The Charboneau case."

"Hmm. I don't suppose you'd be this mushy-brained if she were, let's just say, less than attractive."

He gave her a serious stare. "Yes, she's beautiful, but I'm only interested in doing my job, and catching the creep who kicked her door down and tried to abduct her." He pulled in a breath, watching a slow smile bow Gina's lips.

"Just checking to see if you've caught the bug, too, because in case you haven't noticed, the single men in this department have lost touch with any measure of decorum they may have possessed. It's Miss Charboneau this, and Adelaide that—"

"You're jealous?" Royce followed her into her lab and leaned against the counter.

"No. But my date-night calendar for this weekend is empty. Care to disprove my observation? I'll pencil you in."

"Busy."

"I was counting on you to be immune."

He wasn't immune, but he opened his mouth to quantify a denial.

Gina held up her hand, and the rebuttal stuck in his throat.

"Yes. I have some results on the Charboneau scene."

He clamped his teeth together and smiled.

"Men," she grumbled as she snagged a file from her desk and returned to the counter. "I'll have you know she has turned every one of them down for a date in the past six months. I have no idea why they keep banging their heads against that wall."

A measure of admiration circulated in his brain as he watched her open the file and spread out its contents.

"There were no prints on the duct tape, but I did find some fibers, possibly from a pair of gloves, which would explain why we didn't find any foreign prints on the tape, or anywhere in the house."

She slid the photo of Adelaide's bound hands in his direction, exposing the one underneath. It showed the towel used to blindfold her, but he couldn't keep his eyes off the close-up of her lips that had made it into the top of the frame.

Full and supple, slightly parted. Sexy as hell.

The desire to connect them with his own, and part them even farther with his tongue, streaked through his mind before he could pull it back.

"The footprints from the kitchen floor, and the one from under the studio window, do they match?" he asked, more than ready to refocus his thoughts on the crime scene, rather than the crime's beautiful victim.

Gina flipped the tantalizing photo over with a decisive slap. "No. We're looking at two different sets of footprints. Two different subjects."

"There's no way to tell if they were made on the same night?" Concern laced through him.

"Not unless you're some sort of human surveillance camera. It's just the toe of a shoe, and the only reason I was able to cast it at all is because the overhang protected it from the downpour. Otherwise, it would have dissolved."

Royce straightened and crossed his arms over his chest. "So we've got nothing from forensics except the revelation that there are two subjects out there who are focused on Miss Charboneau. One a brutal assailant willing to kick her door down and take her, and the other a Peeping Tom?"

"I'm sorry, Beckett. I wish I had more to give you."

He tried to calm the frustration that frayed his nerves, and ground worry into his head, but every case was only as good as the evidence left behind by the perpetrator, and the memory of the victim, *if* they survived the ordeal.

Thank God Adelaide Charboneau had.

"You gave it your best shot. Thanks." He flashed her a smile and left the lab.

The clock was ticking. One of the subjects would be back, and when he showed up again, Royce planned to be there.

ROYCE RAISED A CUP OF HOT coffee to his lips and pulled in a sip, watching Adelaide from over the brim as she worked her way along the front veranda watering her flower beds.

If she knew he was keeping watch over her, she didn't respond any differently than she had for the last couple of evenings.

At dusk, she watered, her lights went out at ten and came on at six a.m.

Transfixed, he watched her drop the hose and deadhead a patch of bright pink petunias.

Tucking his finger in the crux of his tie, he pulled the knot down and fingered the top button of his shirt.

Why did observing her always make his temp rise, and his muscles tense?

She bent over, snagged the running garden hose, straightened and flipped back a mass of wavy brunette hair that fell well past her shoulders. Once again she aimed the stream of water and continued to move along the edge of the flower bed.

Royce's mouth went Saharan. Who knew a simple chore could incite the kind of heat he felt assault his body and sink into his bones. At this rate he was no less crass than the boys back at the station, who'd give their pension to be working this case.

Taking a hostile gulp of coffee, he burned the hell out of his tongue. Sputtering, he put the cup in the holder and leaned his head back against the headrest, breaking his line of sight on her while he tried to get his head screwed on straight.

Night couldn't come fast enough, he decided, but it did, and three hours later he watched the lights go out one by one all through the big house.

He glanced at his watch. Ten p.m. on the dot. No wonder

the guys couldn't get a date with her—she was a creature of habit, and probably didn't like to break her routine. For anyone.

Relaxing back, he stared up at the headliner in the car and squeezed his eyes shut tight, then opened them again, blinking away the grit.

The pop of the door handle on the passenger side snapped his head around, just as the dome light came on inside the car. He went for the weapon at his side, and his pistol was halfway out of its holster before he recognized the woman who'd climbed into the car and shut the door.

He dialed back a surge of adrenaline from his veins, reached up and turned off the dome light switch, hoping the unsub wasn't watching from somewhere in the dark. If so, he'd just been made. "Miss Charboneau."

She smiled. An innocent grin he could just make out in the shadows. "Sorry I spooked you, Detective."

So much for a macho response—he didn't have one—but if it had been anyone else but her, they'd be picking their teeth up off the floorboard right now.

"When did you discover I was here?"

"This afternoon, at the station. I went in for a sketch session and overheard the chief ratting you out."

"Yeah, voices carry over there in the marble halls." The air between them was charged, and he glanced over at her in the filtered light coming in from a streetlamp a hundred feet to the south. "I should have told you, but I didn't want you to alter your routine."

"I know." She thrust a brown paper bag toward him. "So I made you a chicken salad sandwich."

Royce caught a glimmer of pride in her green eyes. As he reached for the bag, their fingertips brushed. "My favorite."

She stared at him for a moment, licked her lips and pulled her hand back. "It's the least I could do, considering you're out here watching over me, keeping me safe."

Royce opened the bag, bent on satisfying his hunger, but realized it wasn't for food. He rolled the top of the sack down and set it on the console. "I'm doing my job, Miss Charboneau."

"Call me Adelaide, please."

"Okay. Adelaide. This is a nice break from the action, but you're safer inside your house. I've got a feeling he may be watching right now, and you're here, where he could discover me before I can catch him."

"You're right...of course you're right." She glanced away for an instant and stared into the darkness before refocusing on him. "If you need anything, the key to my door is under the mat on the front porch. Help yourself."

"That's not safe." Worry rocketed through him. "It could be discovered, and he won't break a window to get in next time. You might not have time to dial 911 before he gets to you."

"Don't worry." She reached out and put her hand on his arm for an instant. "I move the key discreetly every couple of days."

A measure of relief coated his nerves, but his worry remained. "How's your ankle?"

"Much better. I'm getting around on it, and it's almost back to normal."

"There's something I forgot to ask you the other night."

She turned her full attention on him.

He pulled in a breath, awed by how beautiful she looked in the shadowy darkness. Shocked by the level of arousal taking his body one degree at a time. Why was he drawn to her with such an unreasonable reaction? A reaction he wasn't able to control?

"The word *behold* was carved in the siding under your studio window."

Her features changed, her eyes narrowed, her lips pulled into a frown, before the look of concern evaporated.

"Does that mean anything to you?"

"No…nothing."

She reached for the door handle. "I'll leave you to it, Detective Beckett. Sorry I disturbed you."

He opened his mouth to speak, but she was already out of the car and vanishing into the deep shadows. Pulling in a breath, he stared at the route she'd taken and watched her cross the street. Real or imagined, he knew he'd upset her. But her reaction to his question was suspect. So why would she hold out on him? Why would she prefer a lie over a truth that could save her life and help him catch her attacker?

The unanswered question pestered him well into the night and right up until the moment a light flickered on in a downstairs window.

Royce straightened in his seat and glanced at his watch. Almost 3:00 a.m. Close to the time her home had been invaded almost a week ago.

Caution tightened the pit of his stomach as he stared at the blade of light slicing through the darkness from the window of her studio.

What could she possibly be doing in there at this time of night?

Movement at the edge of the light sawed through his attention. His heart rate picked up and thrummed in his ears. He could just make out the silhouette of a man, pressed against the side of the house.

The unsub? Had he been there the whole time?

Tension twisted his muscles into knots. Stealth was his only option. He needed to catch the creep. Now…tonight, before he tried to hurt her again.

Reaching down, he snagged his radio and called for backup. He picked up the mini-mag flashlight from the seat next to him, shoved it into his pocket and clipped the portable radio on his belt.

Keeping his focus locked on the subject, he opened the

car door and climbed out. He didn't shut it, but instead left it open a crack. If the subject heard a car door latch, he'd take off like a shot.

He took a low profile, crossed the street and sagged into the shadows next to the sidewalk.

Pausing at the head of the alley, he took cover next to a fence. Royce eased his head out and stared into the darkness. At the other end, a block away, he spotted a car parked at an odd angle under a streetlamp. Did it belong to the Peeping Tom?

Agitation rocked his body and coated his nerves. He pulled back, took the radio from his belt and relayed the location of the vehicle to the uniforms in a low whisper. If it did belong to the suspect, they'd have him before he had a chance to run, or they'd have a plate number to track him with.

Somewhere in the thick night air, he heard an engine turn over. He listened, but couldn't dial in its location as the hum mingled with the tune of the city streets.

The hair on the back of his neck bristled. Warning bells sounded in his head, but it was too late, he'd already stepped out into the open mouth of the alleyway.

The roar of the speeding car's motor sliced into his awareness just as he caught a glimpse of its dark, sleek body fifty feet from where he stood and closing in like a rocket.

Royce lunged for the other side of the alley, the forward momentum driving him onto the asphalt inches from the kamikaze car.

It passed close by, so close it ruffled his hair.

Royce rolled over, pulled his gun and took aim just as the driver of the car tapped his brakes, released and barreled into the distance and out of range.

He'd like to believe that was random, but it didn't stick. Frustrated, he lowered his weapon and came to his feet. He'd gotten the first two numbers on the licence plate, 32, and he recognized the taillight configuration of a Mustang.

He radioed the car's direction of escape and the partial plate number before turning his focus on the lit window as he came around the end of the fence and stepped into the yard, staying in the cover of the bushes.

Surprise rippled his nerves and rooted him in place. The subject still stood in the same spot peering into Adelaide's studio window, his forehead resting on the bottom right-hand pane.

How was that even possible? How did he not hear the commotion from the alley seconds ago and get spooked? He'd heard of fixation, that locked-on tunnel vision in which nothing exists outside the focus, but he'd never seen it in action, not until tonight.

Damn scary. He raised his weapon and edged out of the trees. "Police. Turn around and show me your hands."

The startled subject raised his hands and took a couple of calculated steps back.

Caution ran along Royce's nerves. Only seconds existed between surrender and pursuit, with nothing in between but bullets and mayhem.

Was the Peeping Tom armed and dangerous? He couldn't be sure. "NOPD. Turn around."

The man bolted.

Royce rushed toward him, closing the distance in quick strides, but the suspect dove for the ground at the corner of the house, crawled around it and disappeared out of sight.

He reached the side of the house and flattened against it. Gun raised, he slid along the wall, stopping only briefly to glance in the studio window at what the subject had seen moments ago through the two-inch crack at the bottom of the window shade.

Adelaide was lying on the floor of her studio among a smattering of sketches. He looked for blood, and saw none.

Somewhere in the dark, he heard bushes rustle, followed by running footsteps. Royce pushed away from the house and charged for the backyard. There he found an opening in the foliage and stepped out into the alley. A block over he heard a motor start up and the engine rev.

He bolted to the corner in time to see a flash of the car's taillights, and then it was gone. Pulling the portable radio off his belt, he alerted the squad car to the vehicle's exact direction of travel. With any luck they'd get the plate number and a description of the car.

Royce hurried for the house. Had Adelaide somehow been injured while he sat outside in his car? If so, the subject would have had to be able to walk through walls.

Key...key...under the front mat.

Hurrying up the steps of the front porch, he flipped up the mat and picked up the key. He shoved it into the lock and opened the door.

Was she okay? Had he somehow blown his mission to keep her safe? The string of unanswered questions all ran together in his brain as he rushed down the hall and into the studio.

He dropped to the floor next to her and reached out, touching her warm body.

"Adelaide. Adelaide." He listened to her suck in a startled breath and realized he'd just awakened her.

Her eyes flicked open and she pulled back for an instant. Tears flooded the brim of her lower lashes. She reached out for him.

He pulled her against him, feeling her body tremble.

"Make them stop, Royce. Make them stop." A sob shook her, and he settled into a rocking motion, trying to comfort her.

"What, Adelaide? What do you want me to stop?"

She didn't answer as he stroked the nape of her neck, feeling her go pliant in his arms. Streams of heat entered his body and burned in his veins. There it was again, that inexplicable hypnotic edge of desire present every time he touched her.

"Tell me. You've got to tell me if you want my help."

"It's here…it's all around me."

Now she was talking in riddles, riddles he couldn't understand. Crazy talk, and as much as it pained him, he let her go and sat back, not breaking contact where he held her bare shoulders between his hands. Was she still half-asleep?

"Make sense, Adelaide. You've got to make sense."

She swallowed hard and met his gaze. The veil of drowsiness lifted, and she visibly straightened, shoulders back, chin up.

"It's here." She motioned to the drawings on the floor with a slight tilt of her head. "They wake me up from a dead sleep and I'm compelled to come down here and draw these… these…"

"Pictures?"

"Yes." She looked away and shook her head. "But they're becoming more detailed, more intense. Tonight I was able to give her a face."

For the first time, Royce looked down at the drawings spread out around them.

His mouth went dry and he released her to pick up the nearest one, trying to conceal the creeping layer of revulsion that the sadistic image churned in his gut.

"They're horrific, and I can't get them out of my head."

Glancing up at her, he watched a tear zigzag down her cheek and tried to imagine how the woman in front of him could draw a murder scene that included a posed female body.

"Please, you have to understand. I don't know where they're coming from, they just come." She turned misty green eyes on him and he couldn't resist.

He reached out for her and pulled her against him, feeling the silkiness of her skin under his fingers. Smelling the sweet, spicy scent of her hair. He closed his eyes for an instant to absorb the sensations, but the only thing he saw was the image of a disturbing murder.

What was going on?

He didn't know, but he needed to find out, that was, if he could reconcile the ugly drawings around them with the beautiful woman in his arms.

Chapter Three

Adelaide fidgeted in the padded chair and wrapped her hands around the cup of coffee sitting in front of her on the table. This was her sanctuary inside the police station, a place where she helped innocent victims visualize, describe and mentally relive their nightmare to bring their tormenter back to life and onto an APB sheet.

She took a swallow of her coffee. It was lukewarm. She worked to get it down and leaned back. Detective Royce Beckett would walk into her realm any moment now, and she'd be forced to explain the drawings he'd gathered up off her studio floor last night.

But she didn't have an explanation…at least not one that would make sense to a clear-and-present-danger sort of man like him.

Just the memory of him holding her made her cheeks warm. He made her feel safe, made her want to try to survive what was coming.

A couple of quick knocks, and the door opened. He stepped into the room, sucking the oxygen out of the space, and her lungs, too.

She looked up, catching the full force of his intense, dark-eyed perusal, but she couldn't keep her focus from drifting to the sketches he held in his right hand between his thumb and index finger.

"Detective." A wash of nervous energy rolled over her.

He smiled for an instant. "Adelaide. Nice place you have here." He eyed the room, nodding his head in approval before he returned his attention to her.

"I understand how important it is for you to make victims feel safe. Protected. I'm sure it helps them give you the information you need to sketch their assailants."

She settled back in her chair, feeling the first whisper of fear skitter over her nerve endings. "I like to think so."

He pulled out a chair across from her and lowered himself into it, setting the sketches on the table next to him. That was when she noticed a Polaroid picture on the top of the pile. He picked it up and put it down in front of her.

"I need you to take a look at a snapshot of the man we believe was looking in your window last night. We got his name from a plate check on a car parked a block over from your place. Do you recognize him?"

She reached for the photo, unable to still the quaking of her hand as she picked up the picture and stared at the shot of the man's face.

"Yes. I've worked with him before. This is Clay Franklin. I did a sketch of his mugger a little over three weeks ago, but they haven't caught him yet."

She glanced up to see Royce studying her with an intensity that made her skin prickle.

He broke eye contact, pulled a notepad and pen from his shirt pocket and jotted down some information before he looked back up at her.

"I know the mugger's sketch went out on an APB, and WGNO-TV ran it. Five people have been mugged in the same area, but Clay was the first victim who got a good look at the man's face." She licked her lips and tried to relax, but she knew he was dissecting her, her information, and most assuredly the sketches lying next to him.

"Did he say anything to you? Did he put the moves on you? Give you any indication that he was interested in you?"

"Enough to become a Peeping Tom and spy on me you mean?"

An amused grin tugged at his mouth. "Yes. Enough to watch you on more than one occasion?"

"No." She ran the drawing session over in her mind, sorting for important details she may have missed. "Not at first. But he did take to staring at me profusely once I revealed the sketch of his attacker to him. It made me uncomfortable."

"That's an affliction the bulk of the department's males seem to have in common with Mr. Franklin."

Embarrassment bloomed on her cheeks. "I wouldn't know about that."

His eyes narrowed for an instant, and she wondered about his thoughts. It was true, she'd been approached time and again by the officers of the NOPD, but Detective Royce Beckett was the first one who sparked any interest inside her.

"I'll pull the file and we'll bring him in for questioning. See if his shoe imprint matches the one we found under your studio window the night you were dragged from your home. It doesn't match the ones we photographed on your kitchen floor that night, so it's safe to confirm he wasn't the man who broke in and tried to abduct you. It only quantifies the fact that there are two of them."

Fear bubbled up again, and she worked to push it back from the edge of her thoughts. She couldn't function if she let it escape; it would only send her into a cycle of terror she couldn't defuse.

"Did he leave any evidence at the scene?"

"None that we could find."

Regret welled inside her. If only she'd have seen the man's face. She'd love nothing better than to let her pencil and sketch pad reveal him and land him in jail.

"And then there's this." He reached for the sketch on top and flipped it over. "Do you want to tell me about it?"

Adelaide stared at the disturbing drawing. Her throat constricted. Looking up, she met his gaze. Lying about the drawing wasn't going to work. Detective Beckett possessed more determination and persistence than she'd ever be able to challenge.

"It's a depiction of my death."

Royce rocked forward in his chair. Leaning across the table, so close she could smell the slightest hint of his sultry aftershave. His handsome features were set in dead-serious resolve, and she let his intensity coil around her, drawing her into the emotion.

"You can't mean that," he whispered. "She's wearing your face, but I'll be damned if I believe that's you."

Brushing the stunning sketch with her gaze for an instant, she again raised her eyes to his. "Then be damned, Detective, because that's how I'm going to die."

She dropped her stare back to the haunting image, disturbed by the tone of certainty in her own voice. Certainty, yes, but acceptance? It was the first and best-developed image of the sketches she'd been compelled to draw for weeks now. It depicted her lying faceup in the trunk of a car. Her hands bound in front of her with duct tape. Her hair fanned out around her face. Eyes wide open, lips parted in a silent scream. A deep ugly gash slashed across her throat.

"I believe you saved me from this the other night." She focused on him. He clamped his teeth together, sending a visible ripple of tension along his jawline.

"This will be my fate, Detective, and there's nothing you can do to stop it."

"You can't believe I'd ever let that happen to you, Adelaide."

Hope surged inside her for an instant, but dispersed quickly, dragging her back into a reality she couldn't paddle her way out of.

"I've made peace with it. These things happen. God knows in my line of work, I've drawn the deplorable things one human being can do to another."

She reached for her sketches, but he beat her to them and covered her hand with his.

"Effective immediately, I'm posting a uniformed officer outside your home. This nut job is still out there, and you're not safe until we catch him."

"I'd like my sketches back. They're not part of this investigation." She pulled in a breath, watching Royce's mouth soften, followed by the rest of his features.

"I'm sorry, but I plan to hang on to them for now." He removed his hand from over the top of hers and picked up her drawings, then stood up.

"I want you to go home and feel safe. We're going to catch these people."

"Thank you, Detective. I'm sure you will." *Someday.* She couldn't embrace his assertion because she knew what she knew, and that truly frightened her.

Royce turned for the door and reached for the knob, just as a knock thumped against the wood.

He pulled it open, feeling like an oppressive weight rested on his shoulders and crushed him into the carpet. He'd consider her outlandish claim, but it was too far out there, like shelving two centuries of knowledge only to again believe the sun revolved around the earth, and the moon stood still.

Zoned out, he glanced at Chief Danbury's face. He took a step back. Something big must be going on to drag him out of his office and upstairs.

Friction snapped in the air between them and heightened his interest.

The chief raised his hand and acknowledged Adelaide.

"Miss Charboneau." He motioned Royce out into the hallway and pulled the door closed behind him.

"What's up?" Royce asked.

"I need you to roll on a homicide call that just came in. Detective Hicks and Detective Lawton are already on their way to the scene. A deceased female has been found out in Bucktown on the edge of City Park." He turned and headed for the elevator. Royce fell in next to him.

"It looks like a ritualistic killing. The body was posed. We may have some sort of a serial killer on our hands."

Royce absorbed the chief's information, but it was the word *ritualistic* that played bad inside his head and raised his caution level. That was his take on the disturbing drawings he carried in his hand right now.

Adelaide Charboneau's sketches were of ritualistic-style murders and posed female victims. Four, to be exact, excluding the one she claimed would be her own. But only one of the four victims in the sketches had a face. A haunting face he couldn't get out of his mind.

He tried to relax as they stepped into the elevator, tried to dumb down the persistent feeling of dread growing inside him like kudzu, but the insidious vine had already taken hold, and it couldn't be uprooted.

WATER AS FAR AS THE EYE COULD see blurred Royce's vision as he exited Veteran's Memorial Boulevard, headed due north straight for Bucktown and Lake Pontchartrain. A beautiful view…an ugly place to die.

Deleting his last thought, he sobered, recalling the sketch of Adelaide he'd shuffled into the others and locked in his desk drawer at the station. None of it made sense, at least not within the parameters he used to define the world. How did someone even go about sketching their own murder, much less somebody else's?

Ahead he saw the flashing lights on police units lined up in succession until he could almost believe they disappeared into the flat gray water. On the opposite side of the street he spotted a WGNO-TV van with its occupants in the process of gearing up.

He eased his car in on the tail of the parade, cinched his tie and stepped out of the air-conditioned car straight into a wall of heat.

Good thing cool-on-the-outside Ice Man Beckett was his motto, but he left his jacket on the front seat and headed into the fray, passing five patrol units before he saw Gina Gantz climbing out of the back of the CSI van.

"You came to the circus," she said when she saw him, but she wasn't smiling, and he could always count on her for that.

His nerves pulled tight. "Have you already been to the scene?"

"Yes." She swallowed.

"How bad?"

"The chief has two more technicians rolling in to help me collect evidence."

"Brutal?" he asked.

"Creepy is more like it. No blood, no gore. Just a beautiful young woman, murdered and posed for some sick reason."

Royce took a deep breath and settled in next to her as she walked toward a perimeter of yellow crime-scene tape.

He flashed his badge to the uniformed officer guarding the scene, lifted the crime tape and followed Gina underneath it. Glancing down toward the water, he spotted Detectives Hicks and Lawton standing with several other officers.

His skin was pretty thick. Armored in fact, but it came with the job. It had to.

Hicks glanced up, spotting him as he stepped closer.

"Detective Beckett."

Nodding to the detective who outranked him by a couple of months, he got his first look at the victim.

"Her name's Missy Stewart," Hicks said, glancing down at his notepad. "She's twenty, a student at Tulane, reported missing the day before yesterday by her roommate."

Royce pushed back a rush of anger over the senseless killing and put his detective face on. Cold, hard, analytical thinking solved cases, not emotionally clouded judgment.

He stepped closer, studying the details. "You found her wallet open and displayed next to her body?" It was something missing in Adelaide's sketch.

"Yeah. It wasn't moved or touched by the jogger who found her this morning. We believe it was placed there by the killer." Hicks motioned with a tilt of his head. "You saw her right hand?"

"Yeah." But he didn't need to take a second look. He knew the positioning of the body. Laid out, fully clothed. Long hair fanned out around her face, eyes wide open and fixed on the sky. Legs together. Left arm straight at her side, right arm stretched out, level with her shoulder. Right thumb locked across three fingers, and her index digit pointing in a southerly direction.

"The chief's right. This looks ritualistic in nature. Any idea what her cause of death is, and what the devil this grainy substance is around the body?" Another detail missing in Adelaide's depiction of the crime scene, but she was still four for six.

Gina looked up from her task, reached into her pocket and pulled out a GPS locator for the exact placement reading.

"Judging by the fixed open position of her eyes, my best guess is some sort of drug." She put the GPS button down at the tip of Missy Stuart's finger. "The substance around the body is where this gets creepy. The granules are sodium chloride."

"Common table salt."

"Yes." Gina took the reading. "This has voodoo written all over it, Beckett. Dark magic. I don't believe in any of it, but some folks do and salt plays a role in some of their rituals."

She reached down and picked up the marker. "Are you okay, Beckett? You look like you've seen a ghost."

Ghost? No. A sketch? Yes. Voodoo was a wrinkle he hadn't anticipated, but he planned to confront Adelaide Charboneau and have her try to explain why the dead woman at his feet matched one of her sketches. He wouldn't take any mumbo-jumbo dark magic reasoning for this.

He'd charge her with murder, or at least accessory, arrest her and haul her off to jail.

"Hold on to your hats, folks. There's another tropical storm brewing in the Atlantic. This one has affectionately been named Kandace, and she's packing winds of seventy-five miles per hour. She could reach hurricane status by week's end—"

Adelaide pushed the off button on the TV remote and tossed it onto the coffee table. Two storms were her limit. One packed wind and rain, the other packed a badge and a gun, and enough sex appeal to brew his own weather system.

Why he hadn't blown down her door yet, she didn't know, but she was sure he'd roar in much sooner than Kandace.

The department was abuzz with details about the girl they'd found murdered in Bucktown. Normally it would have been internalized, but the fact that she'd been posed and circled with salt seemed to give everyone permission to speculate on the dark magic details.

She owed her own certainty to some of the telltale details. The victim's pointing finger on her right hand, the fan of hair spread out around her head, eyes wide open. All details she'd been compelled to sketch over and over again.

Buzzed with the jitters, she got up off the sofa and went into the kitchen to make a cup of herbal tea.

Detective Royce Beckett was an intelligent man, a good cop. He'd no doubt done a comparison between the victims in her sketch and the body found this morning.

Adelaide turned on the burner under the kettle, pulled her favorite smiley face mug out of the cupboard and opened the tea canister on the counter, selecting chamomile.

She wasn't an investigator, but she had enough sense to know things weren't going to get better. Not for her...and certainly not for the women in the sketches.

The front doorbell chimed.

Dropping the tea bag into the mug, she braced herself for the grilling ahead. She'd probably do the same thing if she were in his official capacity.

A knot of tension sat heavy in her stomach by the time she reached the front door and glimpsed the shadow of his imposing silhouette outlined through the filmy glass flanking either side of the door.

Hesitation stringed through her, and she went up onto her tiptoes to stare through the peephole, confirming what she already knew. Detective Royce Beckett was here, holding a rolled-up sketch in one hand, and he wasn't happy.

Pulling in a cleansing breath, she stepped back and opened the door.

"Detective." She smiled, even though he didn't.

"We need to talk."

In the background the shrill whistle of the kettle at full boil saved her from the intensity of the moment. "Tea?" she asked over her shoulder as she hurried down the long hallway to the kitchen, hearing the front door close behind him.

"No, thanks. This isn't a social call."

Worry jumbled her nerves as she turned off the stove, lifted the kettle and bathed the tea bag in scalding water. The comparison between the steaming cup and what was coming was just too unsettling, and she set the kettle down on the back burner.

Chair legs raked against the kitchen floor, and she turned around, prepared for the only line of questioning he'd be able to follow.

"I heard about the murdered woman they found out in Bucktown. I'm sorry for the tragedy her family is suffering—"

"Cut the niceties, Adelaide. I've got this." He unrolled the sketch, grabbed a couple of apples out of the dish on the bar where he sat and positioned them on the sketch so it wouldn't roll back up.

Next, he reached into his jacket pocket and pulled out a photo.

She didn't have to ask what it was, she already knew, and for an instant she wanted to curl up along with the sketch, if she could only get the apples off it.

"It's a perfect match, Adelaide." He stared at her across the bar. Her throat tightened. There was sorrow in his dark eyes. Sorrow, remorse…and pain? She wanted to reach out for him. To feel his arms come around her shoulders, to feel his proximity soothe her fear.

"I don't want to arrest you as an accessory, but if you leave me no choice, I'll do it. I need an explanation, and I need it now."

Her gaze locked with his, her knees wobbling as she leaned against the counter for support. "I lied to you when I said I didn't know what the word *behold* meant."

"The one we found carved into the wood under you studio window, presumably by Clay Franklin?"

"Yes." She hesitated, considering the ramification of the revelation. It was a secret she protected, didn't share and certainly hadn't told Clay Franklin about, but Royce needed to know the truth about her.

She pushed back and moved around the counter toward him, feeling the need to be closer. The need to convince him of her innocence. "But he didn't complete the word. It's *Beholder*." She stopped next to him. "I'm what was once known by the now-extinct Materia voodoo sect as a Beholder. I see pictures of assailants coming directly from the mind's eye of the victims I help, and I sketch them."

If her revelation sparked any sort of understanding in Royce, it didn't register on his face. His features were masked, unreadable...hostile?

"Hold on just a minute. You expect me to believe, what? That you see images coming from inside a victim's head, and you can draw them?"

"Yes."

"It'll be a cold day in hell before I ever sign on to mumbo jumbo that outrageous. It doesn't hold an ounce of tangibility, and if it did, then why are these drawings being seen from a killer's point of view?" He pushed his chair back and stood up. "I'm going to act like this bizarre conversation never transpired. I'd like you to do the same."

Disappointment piqued her nerve endings and slammed into her brain with a force that shook her resolve. What had she expected? That her secret talent would be revered? That Royce would accept her revelation and welcome it?

"Please." She reached out for him, laying her hand on his forearm.

Heat arced into her palm and zipped up her arm. Transfixed by the sensation, she stared up at him.

His eyes narrowed for an instant, confirming her belief that he'd felt it, too, she was sure of it, but he nonchalantly pulled back with conviction he didn't feel.

"Someone circled Missy Stuart with a ring of salt. The claim is it has voodoo connotations. If I find out you're involved..."

Fire burned inside Royce as he stared into her luminous green eyes. What the hell was happening to him? He wanted to kiss her, wanted to feel her body tangled up with his, for no other reason than an insatiable desire to touch her.

"There's enough circumstantial evidence to haul you in, but you'd make bail before morning."

Her chin came up, her eyes trained on him, and he found a quality of determination in their green depths.

"I'll come willingly, but it isn't going to change anything. More of them are going to die, Royce. More of the horrific depictions in my drawings are going to happen. It's not if. It's when."

Frustrated, he turned around and headed for the front door, stopping only at the sound of her bare feet tromping along the hardwood right behind him.

"Don't forget your evidence." Her tone was mildly condescending.

He paused and turned toward her, painfully aware of how vulnerable she looked standing in front of him. Her long dark hair tousled around her face. Her eyes bright and wide with anger. Hell, he couldn't blame her for feeling indignant. He would, too, under these circumstances. No one liked to be accused of a crime, much less convicted without a trial.

Backtracking, he pulled a business card out of his pocket and laid it on the table in the entryway. "Officer Tansy is posted in a squad car out front. He's one of the officers being assigned to protect you from 10:00 p.m. to 6:00 a.m."

He reached out and took the offending paper from her hand. "Feel free to call me on my personal cell if you need anything."

Turning, he reached for the knob, opened the door and stepped out onto the porch, pulling it closed behind him. But the soft click of the latch did little to separate him from her. He could still feel her ire as he headed down the sidewalk, motioned to Tansy, crossed the street and climbed into his car.

Adelaide Charboneau was safe for now. But he still hadn't located Clay Franklin for questioning. Using that detail alone, he'd been able to secure her nighttime protection, but there were still twenty-four hours in a day.

A measure of foreboding circulated in his veins like slow-acting poison. He shook it off, fired the engine and drove away.

Chapter Four

For the third time in an hour, Royce stared at the personnel file on his desk. Checking into the background of anyone he suspected of a crime was standard operating procedure, but this file belonged to Adelaide Charboneau, and he couldn't fight the urge to squirrel it away and read it in private somewhere.

Did anything in it allude to her intangible talents? Map out her ability to pull sketches of perpetrators right out of a victim's recall like she claimed she could?

Doubtful, he snatched up the manila folder, stood and headed for the copy room in the basement. To be more precise, the tiny cubicle next to it, with a desk, a chair and a locking door. It was rumored to have been a utility closet at one time, before being commandeered by a former police chief who couldn't seem to get his reports transcribed in the rat race upstairs.

Royce almost ran into Detective Hicks, who nodded and paused next to him. "I got Missy Stuart's autopsy report half an hour ago."

His interest peaked. "Cause of death?"

"Succinylcholine." Hicks's lips pulled into a grim line. "Whoever took her drugged her with the paralytic, posed her body and left her to die at the scene. The medical examiner's report indicates she died of suffocation as a direct result of the drug."

"They use succinylcholine in the medical field, don't they?"

"Yeah. To paralyze a patient for intubation before surgery. If no intubation takes place, the drug paralyzes the muscles of the diaphragm, making it impossible for a person to breathe. They're fully conscious for the duration. It has no sedative properties."

"So the monster who injected her may have stood by and watched her suffocate, paralyzed and unable to fight back?"

"Looks that way." Hicks shook his head in disgust.

Rage soaked through Royce, leaving him more determined to find the sick bastard responsible and put him away.

"I'm working a lead." He squeezed the file in his hand. "We'll get this guy. We have to."

"I'm pounding the halls over at Tulane. Maybe someone saw the person Missy left with."

"We'll catch up this afternoon at briefing?"

"Yeah." Hicks headed for his desk, and Royce hauled it to the stairs, preferring the echo of his shoes on solid concrete to the drone of the elevator.

What kind of person did something that heinous to another human being?

He passed the door to the second floor, paused, jogged back up four steps and exited the stairwell. Moving along the hallway, he stopped and entered the research department.

Megan Lorry looked up from behind her desk. "Detective Beckett. I haven't seen you in here for a long time. What can I do for you?"

It was true. He liked to work his own case research. But voodoo? It was something he considered benign. He had no cause to search for information. Until now.

"I need a summary on a voodoo sect called the Materia.

I'd like to know their origin, customs and rituals if possible, and anything you can find on someone they call a Beholder. I'd like to know what their function was within the sect."

Royce was sure Megan's eyes had glazed over by the time he put his request in writing and left the department for the dark halls in the belly of the station.

If Adelaide claimed to be a Beholder, then he needed to know what he was dealing with, didn't he? Justification. He needed justification for feeling like he did about her revelation. *Skeptical.*

He hit the bottom of the landing, exited through the stairwell door and headed for the cubicle.

Once inside, he locked the door, settled into the chair at the desk and opened the file.

Adelaide Charboneau was educated, beautiful…abandoned?

Shuffling through the contents of the folder, he found a faded photograph. His throat constricted in an odd way as he dissected the fuzzy photographic details of Adelaide's past. She'd been abandoned in a church as a newborn, approximate age, five days old. The grainy picture was a snapshot taken that day. A Sunday morning according to the police report that had been filed by the priest. He'd come in to prepare for mass and found the tiny infant wrapped in a blue blanket, asleep in one of the back pews.

He picked up the photograph, switched on the lamp sitting on the corner of the desk and held the picture under the light.

How had she dealt with her abandonment? Did its psychological effects permeate her life through present day? Had it shaped her, molded her into the person she was? Did it explain her strange claim of being a Beholder? Leave her with an inherent need for attention?

In the bottom right-hand corner of the photo, barely within

the frame, he spotted something. He raised the old eight-by-ten glossy closer to the light, trying to make out the shape.

It was a crude doll.

Strange. He doubted a priest would have a doll on hand to give to an abandoned infant. Intrigued, he put the picture down and rummaged through the reports until he found a listing of any and all items found with her. One thing stood out. Adelaide had been listed as a male infant in the police report, boy Baby Doe number twenty-two. He ran his finger down the list and found the item at the bottom under blue baby booties.

Gris-gris doll.

"I'll be damned." He rocked back, contemplating the discovery. He didn't know much about voodoo, but he did know that a gris-gris doll was a voodoo symbol. But a symbol for what?

Broadening his search, he found a child services report and scanned it. He read the section twice. Adelaide's gender wasn't discovered to be incorrect until after she'd been removed from the church and taken to a shelter. After an appropriate diaper change, it was discovered that the infant wrapped in blue was a girl. Odd. It was almost as if someone, perhaps her mother, wanted everyone to believe she was a baby boy.

Royce's cell phone rang. He pulled it out of his shirt pocket. "Detective Beckett."

"Detective. Justin Blain, Auto Theft Division. I got your report on the black Mustang that tried to run you down last week."

"Did anything come back?" he asked.

"We've got a unit, a dive team and a tow truck en route to Lake Cataouatche. A boater discovered a submerged car in eight feet of water using his fish-finder. It's out at the Westside boat ramp. His kid dove down and got the plate number. It came back to a 2005 Mustang GT, black in color, reported stolen around the same time as the incident."

"Great news. It's about time I caught a break in this case."

"There's more. The kid came up sputtering and claims he saw a hand floating through the back window."

Royce froze, trying to join the ends of a thread that didn't match up. "Westside boat ramp?"

"Yes."

"I'll be right there." He closed his phone, slipped it into his shirt pocket and gathered up Adelaide's history. He tucked it all back into the folder, along with the curiosity it had churned up inside him, and left the cubbyhole.

ROYCE COASTED THROUGH THE laid-back town of Ama, Louisiana, and took the Westside boat ramp road, a narrow strip of asphalt that cut through thick groves of moss-draped cypress and Tupelo gum trees.

He'd been fishing out here with his dad and little sister, Kimberly, as a kid. Not much had changed about the landscape since then.

Tension bunched the muscles between his shoulder blades. Those were good times. Good times right before his sister was abducted.

Royce jammed on the brakes, jolting to a full stop as a couple of deer trotted across the road in front of him and vanished into the underbrush on the other side.

"Close call," he whispered. It was time to exit his walk down memory lane and get focused. Kimberly had survived the ordeal and come home alive. Alive was all that mattered.

Taking his foot off the brake, he stepped down on the gas pedal and drove the last half mile to the lake. He pulled off the road and out of the trees into an open area, where the boat ramp slid into the murky water.

The dive team was already shedding their oxygen tanks,

and a wrecker was wrenching the car up out of the depths via the tether they'd attached.

Royce parked well out of the action and climbed out of the car, seeing the rear end of the Mustang break the surface of the water.

It certainly looked like the tail of the car that had attempted to put him six feet under.

"Are you Detective Beckett?" a uniformed officer asked, coming toward him.

"Yeah."

"Troy Jensen. My supervisor said you'd be en route. He said this vehicle may be the one someone used to try to run you down."

"It could be. The first two numbers on the plate were thirty-two."

Royce watched the trunk of the car make it into the light of day and felt his gut tighten. "Look at that."

The officer followed his line of sight just as a hand flopped back from the rear window with the receding water. "Looks like the kid wasn't kidding. There's a body inside the car."

Royce moved closer, watching the car roll up the boat ramp with water slicking off its silt-covered black paint. What were the odds? Could the corpse inside be the driver who was in the alley next to Adelaide's house that night?

He watched Officer Jensen chock the wheels to keep it from rolling back into the lake and open a rear door.

Water gushed out of the car, pouring onto his shoes and soaking his pants up to his knees.

Jensen stepped back, shaking his head, and pulled a pair of latex gloves out of his pocket. "Joe," he hollered over his shoulder to another officer. "Get CSI down here."

Royce moved closer. "What have you got?"

"Looks like murder. I don't know any sane person who would zip-tie themselves to a sinking automobile."

He studied the spot where the man's ankle had been

secured to the steering wheel. The sheer brutality made his skin crawl.

"Can you pull his wallet?" Royce asked, staring at the contorted position of the body folded over the front seat. It was almost as if the man had been in the back when his leg was pulled over the seat, and his ankle secured. He hoped like hell an autopsy would reveal he was already dead when he hit the water.

"Yeah." Reaching into the back pocket of the man's jeans, the officer worked his wallet out and opened it. "Clay Franklin. Age twenty-seven, 415 Dalton, Metairie. Do you know him?"

Royce almost choked, whether on the rotten stench of the lake mud the car had disturbed, or the fact that he was looking at his only witness.

"Yeah. I've been looking to question him in a case since last week." Alarm fired along his nerves, leaving a toxic residue deposited in every corner of his mind.

Clay Franklin couldn't have been behind the wheel of this car that night, because he was peeping in Adelaide's window.

"I'd like Gina Gantz on this one. She's the best."

"No problem."

He turned and headed for his car to wait for the CSI team to arrive. He needed any evidence Gina and her team could find, and he needed it now.

If Clay Franklin was killed by the same man driving the Mustang that night, then he needed to find a link to Adelaide Charboneau before it was too late.

IT WAS HAPPENING AGAIN.

Adelaide fought the overwhelming sensation and burrowed deeper into her pillow, but the image in her head wouldn't be denied. It came again…and again…stronger…more persistent, until a full picture moved through her consciousness, demanding, pressing...horrifying.

She bolted up in bed, flanking her head on either side with her hands.

The woman's features were clear now. Wide-set brown eyes, dark hair fanned out around her face, the index finger on her right hand pointing in an unknown direction.

"Dear God." She threw back the covers and climbed out of bed. Her body trembled as she pulled on her robe, tied the belt and walked into the hallway.

By the time she reached the studio she was fully awake. She climbed onto the stool at her drawing table and opened her sketch pad.

With decisive strokes she began the process of capturing the woman's image with every sweep of her pencil. Her heartbeat escalated in her eardrums, her breathing hitching up. In a hurried flourish, she finished the sketch, and stared into the face of the next victim.

A shudder racked her body, sending a chill through her that rippled down to her bare toes.

Royce...she had to tell Royce. If there was even the slightest chance they could find the woman before the killer did, she had to take the risk.

He believed she was a freak, she knew that much. This would only cement his skepticism. But what if the woman hadn't died yet? It had taken two days from the night she drew the first victim's face until the day her body was discovered.

She tore the page out of the sketch pad and left the studio, hurrying for the stairs, and the cell phone lying on her nightstand upstairs. A shadow crossed the filmy glass next to the front door, and she paused in her tracks.

Fear grazed her nerves.

Officer Tansy was outside. It was possible he was checking the perimeter of the house.

She took a measured step forward, hanging close to the wall.

Outside, the porch light flickered and went out.

Had she moved the house key from under the mat?

Uncertainty pushed her forward. She didn't plan on sticking around long enough to discover who was outside the front door.

She bolted for the stairs, taking them two at a time.

Behind her in the foyer, she heard the knob rattle back and forth.

Darting into her room, she closed the door.

Not this time. She couldn't let him take her this time.

A degree of overwhelming determination wiggled up her spine. Her gaze locked on the highboy next to the door. She put the sketch on the bed and hurried to the other side of the room. Pressing her back to the heavy piece of furniture, she leaned into it.

It gave against the force and inched along the wall. A surge of energy she didn't know she possessed drove her to push harder, and she didn't yield until the highboy was squarely blocking the door to her bedroom.

He wouldn't just kick it in this time. This time she would keep him out long enough for the officer, or Royce, to catch the bastard, but one piece of furniture wasn't going to be enough and she knew it.

If she could move the dresser, too, she could butt it up against the bed and create an impenetrable barrier.

Pulling the end of the dresser, she swung it away from the wall and around, positioning it between the highboy and the bed.

She picked up her cell phone off the nightstand, and paused

to listen to an array of sounds coming from somewhere downstairs.

He could be inside the house, but she wasn't sure, and she had no clear view of the street, or the officer's car parked at the curb.

A loud crash echoed from downstairs. Her studio?

Was he after the drawings?

Opening her phone, she punched in Royce's cell number from memory. It rang three times and rolled over to voice mail.

"He's here again, Royce. I blocked him out of my bedroom with some furniture for now, but I don't know how long it'll hold. Please hurry."

She flipped the phone shut, and jumped when a punishing blow hammered the bedroom door, followed in succession by another one.

Shaking, she stepped back, leaning against the wall next to the window, listening to his brutal attempts to get in.

Her defenses had to hold. They had to keep him out long enough for help to come. Clutching the phone, she dialed 911. Royce wasn't coming this time. She made peace with that fact, and listened to the operator at the other end of the line verify her information and ask for her situation.

The pounding stopped.

Had he given up?

Maybe Officer Tansy realized there was something going on and had come into the house to help her?

"Stay on the line with me, Miss Charboneau. I'm dispatching an officer to your location."

She dropped her gaze to a sudden flicker of light skimming through the crack at the bottom of the bedroom door.

The earth shifted in surreal time as she watched the tiny flicker settle in the center of her room and burst into flames.

Tossing the open phone onto the bed, she lunged for a pillow, grabbed it and beat the fire down.

Was he crazy? Didn't he know she could die if the fire had spread? Sucking in a gulp of caustic smoke, she fought a violent cough. In the background she heard the whisper of the worried dispatcher talking over the discarded cell phone, but it was the hollow tap of boots on the stairs that drew her scrutiny.

Was he leaving? Please, God, make him leave.

Caution hedged her steps as she tiptoed to the door. But the hammer of reality sent her stumbling back in a panic.

A curl of smoke slid under the door, tangling with the glow of fire dancing outside in the hallway.

She rushed for the phone, scooped it up and screamed "Fire" into the receiver. She was trapped in a prison of her own making.

This wasn't how she was supposed to die.

ROYCE PUSHED THE GAS PEDAL to the floor and shot down Canal Street with an unsaid expletive on his lips.

He'd missed Adelaide's urgent phone call by thirty seconds. Thirty blasted seconds. And she didn't pick up when he called back.

Was she still alive? Or was he too late to save her from a monster determined to have her?

Braking, he roared onto St. Charles Avenue and immediately slowed down, spotting the fire trucks two blocks ahead. His mouth went dry, his nerves spinning off on a twisted tirade of their own.

She'd reached out to him, and he'd failed. He pulled up to the curb, jumped out of the car and ran to the scene, slowing only when he spotted her wrapped in a blanket, standing on the sidewalk next to a fireman.

Relief washed away any remorse still thundering in his head, and he pulled in a breath, but the release of tension was short-lived when he spotted two officers standing next to James Tansy's empty patrol car.

Refocusing his attention on Adelaide, he saw her turn her head in his direction. They made eye contact. Urgency put some hustle in his steps, and he didn't take his eyes off her until he reached her side.

"What happened? Did Tansy apprehend him before he got to you?"

She shook her head. "He tried, but—" She dropped her gaze to the sidewalk. "The guy was too strong. Tansy never made it into the house."

Royce went numb, searching for the answers faster than she could give them. Reaching out, he grasped her by the shoulders and locked his stare on her face, on the smudges of soot across her cheeks. "He set a fire?"

"Yes. When he couldn't get into my bedroom, he—" Her voice broke, and he pulled her into his arms.

"Later. You can give me the details later. Right now you're safe. I'm not going to leave you alone again."

He was caught up in the feel of her; in the midst of all the chaos, he was grounded.

Royce glanced at the fireman over the top of Adelaide's head. "What's the nature of the fire?"

"Arson, judging by the burning containers of paper set on fire throughout the house. She was found clinging to the windowsill half in and half out of a second-floor bedroom window. She'd barricaded herself in the room. We got her down with a ladder and put the fires out before the home was involved. This fire wasn't set to kill her, or destroy the home. It was meant to terrorize, even drive her outside."

"What about the officer posted to protect her? What's his status?"

"EMS rolled to the hospital with him. Someone tried to take his head off with a baseball bat, and damn near succeeded, but he's hanging on."

The fireman turned and headed for his truck, where he paired up with another fireman dragging hose toward the rear of the house.

Adelaide opened her eyes and pushed back from Royce. As much as she liked the security of his arms, she had to warn him. Had to make every attempt to save the woman in her drawing from a horrible death.

"I might know what he was after. I have it right here." She reached into the pocket of her robe and fingered the folded sketch right next to the cell phone that had saved her life again. She pulled the drawing out and handed it to him.

"I sketched this tonight, right before he broke in and came after me. She's his next victim, Royce. Victim number two. We have to find her before he kills her."

Chapter Five

Adelaide toweled her hair and left the sanctity of the tiny bathroom, feeling and smelling less like a chimney, and more like herself again.

Royce and a fireman had escorted her back into her damaged house so she could grab some personal items and pack some clothing, which at the moment was spinning in the washer.

She glanced up at Royce, who paced back and forth in front of the picture window of the safe house he'd taken her to shortly after the fire. Chief Danbury had finally realized the danger Adelaide was in and recommended Royce take over and protect her until the maniac was caught.

The air in the room hummed with tension that snapped the second he saw her. He stopped in his tracks, crossed his arms over his chest and spread his feet wide.

She wanted to collapse under the pressure of his scrutiny, but there was nowhere to run. He was her best line of defense against a killer who seemed determined to have her, and who would ultimately get his wish if her sketch held true.

"Better?" he asked.

"Much." She stared at the files he'd spread out on the coffee table in front of the sofa and dialed in the spot she knew she'd be occupying for the next hour while he picked her brain for details she wasn't sure she had.

That was the problem with skeptical people, they wanted proof, and there wasn't time to dish it out. Another young woman's life was hanging in the balance.

"Have any missing women been reported?" She headed for the galley kitchen and a cup of the coffee she smelled brewing.

"Nothing so far. I've been on the phone with Detective Hicks twice already this morning."

In a bustle of frustration, she opened and closed one cupboard after another in search of a mug, finally giving up to lean against the counter in frustration.

"We have to find her, Royce. We have to get to her before he does."

Royce stepped into the kitchen and took a cup off a rack on the countertop next to the coffeemaker.

Adelaide bit back a sigh and pushed away from the counter.

"Look. I know this is driving you nuts, but we can't find someone who hasn't been reported missing yet." He filled her cup and put the pot back on the warming plate.

"What about getting her picture on the morning news?"

"And sending every woman in New Orleans into a panic? It's a drawing, Adelaide. A piece of paper—"

"Until it's not. Until it's someone's daughter, sister, mother."

Royce turned on her and grasped her shoulders between his palms.

Awareness raged through her body, stealing the last of her already-in-the-tank composure. She stared up into his face, seeing his teeth clamp together briefly before he pulled in a breath. Her skin heated where he touched her and she swallowed hard.

"I'm sorry, Adelaide. I know how much you want to prevent anything from happening to her, but cops don't prevent crimes for the most part. We're minutes away, when seconds count, we arrive in time to clean up the mess, and try to make sure the guilty party pays for what they've done." He released her, picked up the cup of coffee from off the counter and handed it to her.

Reaching out, she took it and gazed up at him, realizing he was frustrated, too. That in his line of work the answers didn't come in crystal-clear form, cut-and-dried, who done it, and you're off to jail to do your time.

"What about Officer Tansy? He had to have seen the man who tried to kill him."

"His condition is critical. He's in a coma. Come on, sit down. I've got something else to tell you."

Worry attached itself to her nerves as Royce steered her to the couch.

"Clay Franklin is dead."

"How?"

"We're not sure of the cause of death yet, but they pulled him out of Lake Cataouatche yesterday in the same car someone tried to run me down with in the alley beside your house."

"The killer who wants me killed Clay Franklin?"

"Maybe, but I've yet to establish anything other than the car as a link between the two men. We have a search warrant for Clay's house. We'll execute it this afternoon."

"I'd like to see Officer Tansy. There's a chance I can pull an image of the creep from inside his head and put together a composite."

She saw Royce tense, saw hesitation set his body and features in stone. "Please," she begged, willing to take it up a notch.

He physically relented before he verbally did. "It can't hurt. We've got nothing." He stood up.

She put her cup on the coffee table and pushed up onto her feet, anxious to get out of the tiny house and back into the world outside. Outside where she could counteract the sensations he churned up in her. Sensations of need and desire she couldn't understand or explain, but they were there, had been from the first time he touched her.

What bothered her the most was the intrinsic feeling they were being driven together by some unseen force. Something outside their power to resist.

ROYCE HATED THE SMELL OF hospitals, had since he was a kid when he watched his little sister recover from the trauma she suffered during her abduction.

The physical trauma at least.

"Room 433." The nurse pointed down the corridor from behind the tall counter of the nurse's station.

"Thanks." He focused on the end of the hallway, on the uniformed cop guarding the door to Jim Tansy's room. A precaution at the moment, in case the killer happened to return for another try.

Royce sobered, sensing Adelaide next to him without touching her. Neither one of them was safe as long as the maniac who tried to kill them was on the loose. The same myriad thoughts had to be bumping around inside her head.

He fought the urge to take her hand. To squeeze it in his own and reassure her that he could protect her.

Royce brushed his jacket aside and showed his badge to the officer guarding the door. "Any change?" he asked, hoping Tansy was alert and talking.

"None."

They stepped through the open door into the private room, almost colliding with a man dressed in khaki and blue, carrying a toolbox and wearing a grungy ball cap that barely concealed his scraggly blond hair. The patch over his left shirt pocket read Maintenance, and the name badge underneath it read Derrick.

"Excuse me," he mumbled, head down, as he sidestepped around them and vanished out into the hallway.

Curious, Royce turned and followed him, watching him walk down the corridor and around a corner. "Was there a problem in here?" he asked the officer.

"Yeah. The television wasn't working. He fixed it."

"I didn't know comatose patients liked to watch TV."

"Doctor's orders. Apparently the constant sound of the boob tube can sometimes help them come out of the coma."

"Huh." Royce turned back into the room, feeling like he'd just been duped. But he wasn't a doctor, what did he know?

Adelaide had pulled a chair next to the bed, and she was already opening the large sketch pad they'd grabbed at an art supply store on their way to the hospital.

"Officer Tansy. I'm Adelaide Charboneau, the NOPD sketch artist." Her voice was pleading...anxious...excited. "I'm here to sketch a composite of the man who attacked you last night."

Royce settled at the end of the bed with his back against the wall. It was a long shot, but a degree of hope pulsed in his head, dulling his skepticism.

"Relax and picture his face for me. Was he clean shaven? Or did he have facial hair? Can you see the contours of his chin and cheekbones? Describe his eyes for me."

Tension flared in his body as he watched her take pencil to paper and begin to draw. He couldn't see the image emerging on the paper, and it was all he could do not to move over for a look. Her process seemed orderly, even reasonable.

An almost inaudible shriek derailed his train of thought. Adelaide launched up out of her chair and dropped the sketch pad as if she were holding a poisonous snake.

"What the..." He pushed away from the wall and reached out for her. She stepped into his arms as he stared down at the grotesque face she'd drawn in the center of the pad.

"What is that?"

"I don't know, but that's what he saw."

Doubt raced through Royce's brain, erasing the progress he'd made in believing in her claims.

Beep. Beep. Beep. An alarm on the machine at the head of Tansy's bed went off.

Royce stared at the monitor, at the heart rate line spiking across the screen. It went flat, setting off another alarm, a high-pitched hum.

Officer Tansy was dying.

The officer on duty bolted into the room with a couple of nurses right behind him. One of them turned and raced back out into the hallway. "Crash cart 433."

Within seconds the room filled to capacity with medical staff, all scrambling to save his life. Royce picked up the sketch pad from the spot where it had been kicked into the corner in the commotion and pulled Adelaide out of the room and into the hall.

Every muscle in his body was rigid by the time they reached an empty waiting room across from the nurse's station and ducked inside.

"Adelaide, what is going on?"

She dropped into a chair and stared up at him. "That's what he saw last night. I can't explain it."

Royce sat down in the chair across from her, holding the sketch pad in his hands. "You have to tell me what this is."

She reached for the drawing.

He handed it to her and she studied the image.

"My best guess is it's a Songe mask of some kind. They're rumored to be worn over the face during some voodoo ritual ceremonies. This one would have been worn by a male in the hierarchy. The size of the center crest from the forehead to the crown determines the magical power of the mask, and the man who wears it."

Royce didn't like the sound of that. Now they could be dealing with some sort of nut job who thought he had magical powers while he hid behind a gruesome mask.

Sick bastard.

"How do you know this stuff?" It was a legitimate question in his mind. This wasn't information that came at a person during the normal course of a day, so how and why did Adelaide Charboneau have it?

"I took a semester of cultural anthropology last year before I joined the department."

"Was that to get an understanding of your…talents?"

She glared at him. "Yes. I was curious about my ability, and needed an accepting environment in which to explore it, and to answer my own questions."

"Any idea what sort of ritual this mask is used in?"

She glanced at it, and he witnessed a repulsed shiver. "None, but it could be almost anything, from a reproductive ritual, to a blessing over a newborn child, to a death mask."

"Wait. These masks are worn during sex?" Her cheeks roared to a shade of pink he found beyond sexy.

"No. Just in the ritual dance beforehand."

Oh, hell. "You took that course at Tulane?"

She glared at him and raised her chin. "You've been combing my personnel file, haven't you?"

"Yes. I'm being thorough. I'd be negligent in my duties if I left anything to chance."

The frown on her face deepened into disgust he could feel in the air around them.

"While we're on the subject, I found something interesting in the photograph taken of you on the morning you were discovered abandoned in the church."

Her features softened, and he instinctually wanted to brush her shoulder with his hand. "In the bottom of the frame there was a gris-gris voodoo doll. Do you still have it?"

A humorless chuckle rumbled in her throat. "That was thirty-three years ago. There was no doll." Her jest was well executed, but her eyes went wide with surprise.

"You didn't know about it, did you?" She flinched, and

rocked back in the chair where she pulled in several deep breaths.

"No. My adoptive parents never told me about a gris-gris doll."

He suddenly felt like a jerk for laying the information on her uncensored. "I'm sorry."

"Is it locked up in an evidence facility somewhere?"

"Not that I know of." *Where would something like that go after the fact?* "It was most likely turned over to your adoptive parents, along with your other belongings."

Her green eyes took on a misty quality he could almost interpret as reminiscing. "It must have been left with me by my birth mother. That would mean that my mother still might have it."

"Anything's possible."

"Will you go with me to get it?" she asked.

He watched a hopeful smile part her lips. Lips he willfully wanted to taste. There it was again, an insatiable need he'd been able to control up to this point, but not this time, not anymore.

"Yes."

The room around them fell away. He came to his feet at the same time she did. Their gazes locked on one another in a heated exchange that could singe brimstone.

"What the hell." He pulled her against him, feeling the satisfying jolt of contact.

She raised her face to his, her eyelids closing in seductive submission.

Inches separated them, then centimeters, until he brushed her mouth with his. Heat blasted his senses. He deepened the kiss, spurred by a moan of pleasure from deep in her throat.

Need drugged him, turning his thought processes upside down. He locked his arms around her, and parted her lips with his tongue. Damn, she tasted sweet. He gorged on her, breathing her in, dissecting her sexy flavor, zoning out on the smell of her heated skin as it teased his senses mercilessly.

Primal need pulsed in his groin, turning him rock hard, before a measure of rationalization slammed him back to earth.

He pulled away, breathed in and staggered back, watching Adelaide's eyelids flick open in drunken surprise.

She melted into the chair behind her. "What was that?" she asked, staring at him, her breath coming in little puffs.

Unsettled, and more than a little uncomfortable, Royce lowered himself into the chair across from her. He didn't have a logical explanation for what had just happened between them. He fell back on his training.

"Stress. It can make you do things you wouldn't ordinarily do. We've both been under pressure with this case, and having your attacker still at large, well…" If she was buying his lame excuse for kissing her, it didn't register on her face.

About to attempt a second try at a reasonable explanation, he was interrupted by the officer guarding Tansy. He stepped into the waiting room.

"I thought you'd like to know, Jim is stable for now. But they don't know what caused him to code. They're moving him into a secure room in the ICU."

Royce stood up. "Thanks for the information."

"You're welcome." The officer nodded and disappeared into the corridor.

He glanced at his watch. "Let's head back to the station. We're executing the search warrant on Clay Franklin's house in an hour."

Adelaide stood, feeling her knees wobble for an instant before they locked beneath her. She'd never been kissed like that before. The lip-lock had a transcending quality that left her feeling as if she'd somehow been there, and not been there; it was as if someone else had controlled it.

"I'm going to search missing person's reports for the past

couple of days. Maybe we'll get lucky and find the woman in my drawing."

She headed for the door and stepped out into the hallway, aware of Royce next to her as they moved down the corridor, aware, too, of the way he reached for her elbow, withdrew and reached again, finally pressing his hand against the small of her back as they entered the elevator.

He was hesitant, so was she, but one fact stuck with her. She had enjoyed kissing Detective Royce Beckett immensely, perhaps more than she should have, considering they had a professional relationship.

Still, stress had its advantages. Or was it the release?

ADELAIDE LISTENED TO THE HUM of the car's tires on the asphalt as she stared at the southern horizon through the windshield.

They hadn't spoken a word to one another since they'd climbed into the sedan for the drive back to the station.

A measure of foreboding latched onto her emotions as she studied the bank of black clouds heading up tropical storm Kandace's siege on the city. The storm was on track to make landfall by day's end, and even though they wouldn't receive a direct hit, the rain bands could wreak havoc.

She glanced over at Royce behind the steering wheel, wearing a grimace, and she suddenly wanted to see him smiling and laughing instead of locked in cop mode. She took things pretty seriously herself as a rule, but he bordered on the extreme. What drove him? What made him put his badge on every day and show up?

"If you have something to say, please do it." He cocked his head for an instant and looked at her before turning his attention back to the jam-packed traffic on I-10.

"I was just wondering if you ever smile."

He snorted and grinned, showing her a quick flash of white teeth. "Like that?"

"Yes, it's a start, but since we've been joined at the hip by Chief Danbury, and we'll be spending all our time together, you'd do well to lighten up."

A true expression of humor rumbled up from his throat, and Adelaide listened to him chuckle. It had a softening quality that clung to her spirits, raising them exponentially.

"That wasn't so difficult, was it?"

"No." He flipped on the blinker and exited the freeway. "This job beats you down. I've seen enough horror to last me a lifetime—"

"Then why do you do it?"

He pulled in a breath, but remained quiet, almost melancholy from her vantage point.

"My adopted sister, Kimberly, was abducted when she was five, and taken for three days."

"Oh, no."

"She came home alive, but damaged." He cast her a sideways glance that stirred up her sympathies.

"Did they catch the perpetrator?"

"No. He's still at large all these years after the incident because I couldn't describe him to the police with enough accuracy that they could find him."

"You were there when it happened?"

"Yeah. I was six years old. The kidnapper popped the screen off our bedroom window, climbed in and took her. I woke up and got a face-to-face look at the man. It could have been me. It should have been me."

Adelaide's heart squeezed in her chest. Survivor's guilt? "You can't mean that."

"I'm not certain anymore. It was a long time ago. I do know that because of me, her abductor is still out there. He could still be taking kids for all I know because I couldn't help."

"You're helping now." She met his gaze with her own and smiled. "That's why you do what you do. You help people, Royce. You come when they call…like you did for me."

"You make it sound a lot more noble than it really is."

"I can help you."

He braked at the end of the off ramp, waiting for the light to change. "Help me?"

"The image is still inside your head, isn't it?"

"Always."

"I can release it, if you'll let me." She waited for his response, but it didn't come until they pulled into the parking lot at the station and climbed out of the car.

"I'll think about your offer," he said as he guided her into the department.

Hope churned inside her at the prospect of tackling his demon. Heck, she was already picking up on the image leaking from his memory.

Discomfort flooded through Royce like a dam break, but the worst part was his uncertainty about its cause. He didn't know if it stemmed from her willingness to sketch his sister's abductor, or the disturbing fact that he was beginning to believe she really could.

Red faced and irritated, Chief Danbury stood at the front desk, spotting them immediately.

There was trouble, Royce knew it the instant they made eye contact. "Hey, Chief. What's up?"

He studied Adelaide for a moment before facing Royce. "We just took a missing person's report on a young woman named Wendy Davis. She vanished from a shopping center out in Jefferson Heights day before yesterday."

Caution set up shop in the pit of his stomach. "Have we got a photo for an APB?"

"Yeah. I just put it through on the wire. A copy along with the report will show up on your desk in a few, or you can look at it in the communications room right now."

"Thanks, Chief."

"Don't thank me, just find her." He turned and headed for his office.

"Do you think it's her?"

"I don't know. But we'll do a comparison to the drawing you sketched last night. I have it right here." He dug into the back pocket of his slacks and fished out the folded drawing. It still smelled like smoke, and the acrid scent reminded him of how close Adelaide had come to death last night.

"Come on." He pointed her toward the communications room and followed her inside.

An officer was just removing the photograph from the APB fax when they reached the counter.

"Detective Beckett, homicide division. I need to take a look at that photo."

"Sure." He snagged it from the tray and handed it to Royce. "Make sure it gets back to the chief, or my tail's in a knot."

"Not a problem." But there was a problem, a huge problem, a murderous problem.

Royce stared at the picture of a pretty young female, age twenty-three, with wide-set brown eyes and long dark hair.

The victim in Adelaide's sketch and the missing woman were one and the same.

Chapter Six

Adelaide's heart rate climbed, her breathing ramping up with excitement as Royce pulled in next to a black-and-white police car in the driveway of Clay Franklin's house.

She'd never been in the field before. Never experienced the rush of adrenaline she was sure Royce and his fellow cops felt every day of the week.

"Put these on," he said, slapping a pair of latex gloves into the palm of her right hand. "You're only here as an observer. Look, don't touch."

She nodded and took the gloves. A measure of her excitement subsided. "If I see something of interest—"

"You call me." He stared at her and she allowed her gaze to slip to his lips as she recited his look-don't-touch mantra. "The place could be chock-full of evidence. If you compromise it, it can't be used in court."

"Clay is dead."

"Exactly. His autopsy showed that he didn't drown, he died of blunt force trauma to the head. If he was killed here, we need the physical evidence to catch his killer, or at least, an evidentiary link to whoever did it."

"Understood."

"Good." He flashed her a smile that could melt the polar ice caps and climbed out of the car.

Being under the watchful eye of Detective Royce Beckett

was going to be a lot harder than she'd ever imagined. She got out of the car and fell in line behind him as they approached the front door of the little square house, right behind a pair of uniformed cops with a battering ram.

A sudden chill caressed her body, and she instinctually glanced behind her, feeling a jolt of uneasiness glide down her spine.

The house was fairly secluded, surrounded by moss-draped oak trees, and not in the best part of town.

Clay Franklin was a Peeping Tom, and a sicko, who'd robbed her of her privacy. She understood that, but what she didn't understand was the overwhelming sensation of being watched right now.

It crawled through her brain and settled at the base of her skull. She looked around again, shrugged her shoulders a couple of times and stopped next to Royce.

The officer tried the knob.

Locked.

Next, the heavy equipment came to bear on the rickety front door, and with a single swing of the ram, the latch caved and the door shot open.

"Police!" The officers entered the house, and exited moments later. "It's clear, Detective."

"Take the outside perimeter, check the trash cans, the garage out back. Anything that looks suspicious, I want to see it." Both officers nodded and moved past them, then took off in opposite directions to search the perimeter of the house.

A white van pulled up in front of the house, and CSI Gina Gantz climbed out and rounded the front of the vehicle with a camera on a strap dangling from around her neck. She headed straight for them.

"You'd think I was the only CSI tech in the department, as much as you request me, Beckett." A broad grin pulled her lips back from her teeth, and her focus trained on Royce alone.

Irritation zinged across Adelaide's nerves. Gina Gantz was openly flirting with him.

Taking a sideways glance, Adelaide tried to establish whether or not he was reciprocating, but she had to admit she understood why Gina did it. Detective Royce Beckett was a good-looking man, from his close-cropped dark hair and ripped body, to his sexy brown eyes, that narrowed as he studied her with an intensity that could boil water.

"You have to put them on, Adelaide, or you can't enter the scene."

Snapped back into reality, she quickly pulled the latex gloves on, feeling like an inept schoolgirl caught staring at a popular jock.

"Sorry, it's my first time out on a search warrant."

Royce cracked a smile, amused by her out-of-sorts demeanor. "Relax. We're just going to have a look around."

Behind them, Gina cleared her throat, and he realized she'd said something to him earlier, but he didn't know what. "Let's do this," he said, stepping through the open door into the living room of the home. He didn't need distractions. Not now, not when other people's lives hinged on his ability to do his job with a clear head.

Adelaide's proximity made it anything but clear.

Sobering under the weight of his analysis, he ground to a stop in the middle of the room. Caution riled the edge of his nerves as he turned toward the wall behind the front door.

"I'll be damned." He stepped closer to the wall and the collage of pictures taped to the plaster.

He heard Adelaide's quick intake of breath right behind him. "What is this, what do they mean?"

"Obsession." He stared at the hundreds of pictures of Adelaide, taken at various times of day. Each one cut out and mixed with the rest. "It matches his MO as a Peeping Tom. Can you identify when it started?"

She stepped closer and studied the pictures. "I sketched the composite of the man who mugged him, about a month ago."

He watched her tilt her head to the side and narrow her eyes. "Looks like this has been going on for at least that long. See this one?" She pointed to a shot of her watering her flower bed.

"Those are my alyssum. The purple was just beginning to bloom about a month ago."

"So the catalyst for his obsession started after you sketched his mugger?"

"Looks that way."

The intrusive click and flash of the camera behind them reminded him they weren't alone in the room.

Taking hold of her elbow, he steered her out of frame, into the kitchen and out of earshot. "Do you think he knew you were special?" It didn't come out like he planned, but he pressed on. "He's probably the one who carved the word *behold* into the side of your house. He must have figured it out."

"It's possible, but I do everything I can to keep it a secret. Still, he did look at me sort of strange when I revealed the drawing. He tried to backtrack on some of the details after the fact."

"Can you be more specific?" Royce asked, studying her with an intensity that almost felt like a caress.

"It was almost like he didn't want me to draw a true depiction of the man who brutally assaulted him in an alley in the French Quarter and stole his wallet. If memory serves, he'd been forced to file a report only because Officer Brooks found him within seconds of the attack and called an ambulance, and since he, too, had caught a minor glimpse, Brooks needed Clay Franklin to give the details, or the suspect would go unidentified."

"What if he knew his mugger, and feared retaliation if he

identified him? That could explain why the accurate sketch alerted him to your abilities."

"Yes, but not how he knew what they were. What I am, and what I can do."

One of the officers stepped into the kitchen.

Royce turned toward him. "Did you find anything?"

"We found some sort of crushed mask on the floor in the garage, and the place is wrecked. A struggle of some sort definitely took place out there."

Royce turned and headed for the front door, followed by the officer, Adelaide and Gina.

Caution slipped into him as he stepped through the narrow doorway into the remodeled detached garage. A twenty-by-twenty-foot structure that had been converted into a man-room, complete with a TV, now lying facedown on the floor, and a mini-fridge that hung open exposing a six-pack of beer with two cans missing. A single light fixture hung from the ceiling, and in the middle of the floor was a Songe mask.

Adelaide's breath caught in her throat. Taking tentative steps forward, she stopped, bent over and stared down at the ugly mask that seemed to stare back.

It was splintered in half, split down the middle by a forceful blow of some kind. But even the damage couldn't distort its grotesque features.

A chill piqued her senses, sending a rush of fear deep into her brain.

"Any idea what it means?" Royce asked from next to her.

She straightened. "There's no high ridge crest on this one. Its magic isn't powerful."

"Franklin was a bit player?"

"I don't know." She turned to him, needing to feel his arms around her. She squelched the insistent urge. "Whoever tried to kill Officer Tansy was wearing a mask with a high ridge on the crown. This one doesn't qualify. We need an appointment to see my cultural anthropology professor, Charles Bessette. He might be able to give us answers about the mask's symbolism and magic."

"Bag it, Gina. See if we can obtain a DNA sample from around the mouth. We need to know if Clay Franklin ever wore it."

"I'll get it processed and tagged." Gina left the garage, and the officer followed, leaving them alone in the suffocating afternoon heat that infused the dingy room, even though she was ice-cold.

Royce reached for her.

Adelaide didn't resist; she didn't want to, and only the feel of his arms coming around her chased the formidable chill from under her skin.

"Officer Tansy was attacked by a man in a mask. Clay Franklin was already dead by then. There are more of them out there if we can just make some connections."

His grasp on her tightened.

She closed her eyes, but the images behind her lids only reinforced what she already knew.

There was nothing magical about the crude wooden mask carved into a devilish face, with bulging red eyes, parted by narrow slits for *human* eyes to see out of. Thick lips pulled back over jagged teeth, its hideous features meant to terrorize for some unknown reason.

No...the evil behind this mask was flesh and blood.

ROYCE PULLED OUT OF EXCHANGE Alley onto Conti Street, slowed and took a left onto Royal.

Adelaide was silent on the passenger seat next to him, a fact that worried him. She'd never mentioned how her relationship with her parents was, but it was none of his business anyway.

He braked hard at the corner of Royal and Iberville. The

sultry notes of a jazz classic emanated from a trio playing their instruments in the parking lot on the corner.

"Do you like jazz?" he asked, keeping his eyes on the band of tourists crossing the street in front of them, wearing flame-orange T-shirts.

"Yes. You?"

"Most of it."

She looked over at him and smiled, setting his emotions to a jazzy beat of their own that he could no longer silence. He liked being in close proximity to her.

"Your parents live in Destrehan?"

"Yes. Get on I-10 West, then I-310 South."

"I know where it is." He glanced up into the rearview mirror at a dark blue sedan three cars back. "I use to catch catfish out there."

"And you don't anymore?"

"No time for it." Royce pulled through the intersection, cruised a block and stopped at the light on Canal Street. Looking in the review mirror, he watched the lead car behind him pull into a parking slot, leaving a single car behind them, including the blue sedan.

The light turned green, he accelerated and the car directly behind him peeled off onto Canal. He made the other side of the intersection and coasted down St. Charles Avenue, with the blue sedan right behind them.

They were being followed?

He didn't use his blinker. At the corner of Poydras and St. Charles, he took a quick right and sped up.

The blue car followed suit and made the turn, right behind him. "Don't look back, but I think we're being followed."

"That doesn't surprise me," Adelaide whispered from next to him. "I've been feeling it since we got to Clay Franklin's house."

"And you didn't say anything?"

"You're the cop."

Amusement jolted his sense of humor, which seemed to be on life support lately. "You believe we were followed from there?"

"Maybe. I just know I felt like we were being watched."

"Let's find out." Royce braked, and turned back onto St. Charles. Accelerating, he took the left ramp and blended into the stream of traffic on I-10 West. "We'll try to shake him at the 610 merge."

His pulse rate ticked up as he pressed the gas pedal to the floor and wove through traffic.

The dark blue car hung with him. Farther back now, but still following.

Royce moved over into the fast lane and watched the speedometer climb to seventy-five miles per hour. In the distance he saw the 610 merge.

Staying in the fast lane, he made the sweeping loop, then cut across six lanes of traffic and zipped down the Monticello Avenue exit on the other side.

A quick glance at Adelaide confirmed what he already knew, judging by the tiny squeal his stunt had elicited from her moments earlier.

"If it's okay with you, we'll take Airline Highway out to the 310."

"Good idea." She cleared her throat and sat a little taller in the seat.

ADELAIDE'S NERVES WERE A jumbled mess by the time Royce pulled through the expansive iron gates that barred anyone who might dare to drive up the paved approach to the mansion uninvited. She loved her parents dearly, but enjoyed the distance she'd been able to establish between them, both literally and figuratively, since learning about and developing her talent. Her mother was a proper lady, had raised her in the same vein.

"This is a very nice place." Royce braked in the circle driveway and turned off the car.

"Thank you for driving me out here." She turned slightly so she could look at him. "I've never been very good at rocking the boat."

"You're welcome, and I doubt you're going to end up getting wet. Truth has the power to stir the waters, and calm them sometimes. You'll do fine."

She reached for the door handle and climbed out of the car, pondering his words. It was true, the truth was the truth; it could be told, or covered up, but it would always remain the truth.

Her parents must have had their reasons for neglecting to tell her about the gris-gris doll. She sucked in a deep breath and met Royce in front of the car.

The sound of the front door closing with a decisive click pulled her attention to the front gallery and her mother as she moved along the railing, spotting them standing in front of the vehicle.

"Adelaide. Dear." She waved as she moved forward and descended the wide stairs, striding across the cobbled driveway to where they stood.

"How are you?" she asked, pulling her into her arms. A moment later she stepped back and smiled. "I've got a work crew slated to begin on the St. Charles house next week. They're going to make it as good as new for you, darling."

She glanced at Royce. "You must be Detective Beckett. My daughter told me about you. Thank you so much for looking after her."

"Just doing my job, ma'am."

She took Adelaide's hand and led her toward the stairs. "Your father is away on business. I took the liberty of having Benet make you some of your favorite finger sandwiches."

"Thank you, Mom, but we're not planning to stay long."

Chloris Charboneau paused at the base of the landing and let go of her hand. "What is it, dear? Is something wrong?"

Adelaide felt the air lock in her lungs, but the feeling of Royce next to her bolstered her courage. "There's something I need to know." She stared into her mother's bright blue eyes.

"In the course of the investigation, something has surfaced. There was a doll...Mom. A gris-gris doll found with me in the church."

Her mother's face blanched, making her eyes appear bluer in the process.

"I need the gris-gris doll, Mom. It's important."

Chloris took her hand again, and Adelaide felt her mother trembling as she moved her up the stairs and onto the gallery. "Please tell me you still have it." Mustering gumption she didn't know she had, she pulled up short, braking her mother to a stop. "I need to know...please."

When Chloris turned toward her, there were tears collecting on the brims of her eyelids. "Yes, dear. I still have the doll. For some reason I couldn't dispose of it, even though God knows I tried many times. But I knew this day would come. In fact, I've dreaded it."

Adelaide brushed her hand against her mother's shoulder. "I'm sure you have your reasons for keeping it from me."

A brief flash of embarrassment crossed her features and pulled her gaze down. "It is a voodoo symbol, Adelaide. Your father and I did not want that stigma to follow you through your life. I raised you to be a proper lady, and we only wanted what was best for you."

Her emotions flared, raw and tender, but she reached out and hugged her mother. Tamping down a surge of anger that bubbled across her nerves. She had every right to be angry. She'd been deprived of a pathway to the woman who'd given birth to her. A pathway that had obviously frightened Chloris Charboneau into hiding it.

Adelaide pulled back. "You have been, and always will be, my mother. You didn't give me life, but you gave me one."

She reached out and took Adelaide's hand, giving it a firm squeeze. "Come inside, dear. I'll fetch it for you. I've kept it in the cedar chest all these years."

Looking over the top of her mother's head, she made eye contact with Royce and watched a slow smile take his lips. He was right about the truth. Seeking the doll seemed to have released her mom from the guilt of having kept it secret all these years, and for that she was grateful.

AN HOUR LATER, HIS BELLY FULL of watercress sandwiches, Royce opened the front door for Adelaide.

"Thank you, ma'am."

"Please, call me Chloris, and do come back again."

He nodded his appreciation and followed Adelaide out onto the gallery, closing the door behind him.

The air outside had thickened while they'd been inside, and the unseemly presence of dark rain clouds warred unabated with a scrap of blue sky overhead.

A gust of wind ruffled his hair and made him squint to see. "We're going to get soaked."

Reaching out, he took Adelaide's hand and hurried her down the stairs from the gallery, feeling the first raindrop splat on his forehead before they reached the bottom step, then another one, and in the span of a second, the clouds opened up.

Keeping his focus on the car, they made a run for it.

Somewhere in the distance, he heard a loud crack.

A sting burned across the flesh of his left upper arm.

Realization followed, swift and accurate.

Gunfire.

He dove for cover next to the car, taking Adelaide down with him.

Adelaide hit hard, the air pushed out of her lungs. Dazed,

she rolled over trying to make reason out of nothing, but the sight of blood, dark red and spreading into the fabric of Royce's shirtsleeve, made everything clear.

"Keep your head down," he yelled over the drone as he pulled his cell phone out of his pocket. "Someone just took a shot at us."

Another pull of the trigger, another shot echoed from somewhere nearby, and a slug tore into the sedan, shattering the glass in its path and sending a crystalized shower down around them.

A scream bubbled in her throat, but she held it in, staring at the bullet wound on Royce's upper arm as he punched in 911 and raised the cell phone to his ear.

Worry tensed her muscles, twisting them into knots.

"Detective Royce Beckett, New Orleans PD. There are shots being fired at 9155 Charboneau Court, Destrehan. We are pinned down next to our vehicle. Request officer assistance. ETA?" He got the answer and closed his phone, slipped it back into his pocket and drew his weapon.

Adelaide absorbed the shock of the situation. Royce had been shot. Someone wanted them dead.

"They're ten minutes out. Do you think you can hang on?"

Another slug ripped into the rear of the car and sent her control haywire. She swallowed hard and focused on him, clinging to a measure of his calmness under fire. They were going to get through this. Weren't they?

"Do I have a choice?"

He shook his head, and she flinched as bullet number four took out the rear window with a loud pop that jarred her teeth. The gravity of the situation wiped out the safety zone she'd mentally erected around herself, Royce and the car keeping them from being riddled with bullet holes.

Another shot tore into the rear quarter panel.

"He's on the move. He could be trying to flank us." Alarm

bristled Royce's nerves and throttled him into action. Help would never arrive in time, and his pistol was no match for a rifle.

"Move." He took Adelaide by the upper arm and pushed her forward in front of him, protecting her with his body.

Snaking around the front bumper of the vehicle, he pressed her down onto her belly and motioned underneath the car, glad when she didn't protest, and slid in under the sedan, out of the line of fire.

Raising slightly, Royce crept forward and snagged a glance around the quarter panel on the driver's side, just in time to see a man clad in dark clothes dart behind a moss-covered pine a hundred feet behind the car.

He pulled back, gauging his line of attack. A warning shot drilled into the tree might convince him there would be a price to pay if he chose to fight. But he was still out of range, and short of rushing him without cover—a stupid idea—he'd have to wait until the shooter came closer to get a round off.

The rain abruptly stopped.

Royce glanced up at the sky for an instant, swearing he could hear the sound of sirens.

Caution pulled his nerves taut as he leaned out for a look, but the shooter had heard them, too, and he was bobbing and weaving as he made tracks through the heavy brush in the opposite direction, a rifle slung over his shoulder.

"It's clear, Adelaide. You can come out," he said over his shoulder, but she had already crawled out from under the car. Keeping his pistol ready in case the thug changed his mind, he put his arm around her and pulled her close to him.

"He shot you," she whispered.

"It's just a graze. It'll heal."

"Thank God you're both okay!" The sound of Chloris's voice brought his head around as a squad car rolled up the driveway, followed closely by another one.

Was it possible the driver of the dark blue car that tailed them out of New Orleans was also the sniper who'd just tried to kill them?

How in the hell had he found them?

Worry latched onto his thoughts as he tried to make sense of it, but he would have to do it soon before anything happened to the woman in his arms.

A woman who confused his emotions and spun him in knots he couldn't untie.

A woman he suddenly needed more than air.

Chapter Seven

Adelaide tried to get comfortable on the sofa and focus on the television in front of her, on the silly late-night show whose host hadn't moved her laugh-o-meter once tonight.

Behind her at the breakfast bar rimming the kitchen she could hear Royce shuffling through papers in the file he'd picked up at the station on their return from Destrehan. The man who'd taken shots at them had gotten away, without so much as a trace. So much for Locard's law, "Every contact leaves a trace."

Agitated, she stood up, picked up the TV remote from the end table and pressed the off button. She felt totally useless at the moment, trapped in the safe house with Royce.

Did he feel it, too?

She glanced at the picture window, at the rivulets of rainwater tracking down the glass, at the darkness beyond.

Wendy Davis was out there somewhere. Cold, wet, alone? A shudder vibrated at the base of her neck and quaked over her.

She put the remote down and went into the kitchen, casting a quick glance at a shirtless Royce, who was absorbed in the paperwork spread out in front of him.

"Would you like a cup of tea?" she asked, turning on the gas under the kettle and glancing at the time on the oven clock. It was almost midnight. Well past her bedtime.

"No, thanks."

She opened the cupboard next to the stove and pulled a tea bag out of its box. Taking a cup off the rack, she dropped the bag in and turned around. She watched him sitting under the pendant light over the bar.

"Are you planning to stay up all night working on the case?" She tried like crazy not to focus on his broad shoulders and bare chest. Instead she trained her focus on the thick white bandage around his left upper arm, the one that covered his ample biceps....

"Maybe. There are so many angles to consider, and I'm having a difficult time staying on top of all of them."

"Because you're babysitting me?" She considered him in the warm light shining down from the fixture. It made his skin look bronze and it hot-wired her emotions.

"That's my assignment, and judging by what has transpired in the last couple of weeks, it's a good thing you've got me keeping watch over you."

The kettle whistled, and she broke eye contact, feeling a surge of warmth jettison the tingle of guilt nipping at her conscience. She was the center of his attention, when he could be out trying to find Wendy Davis.

She turned off the burner, picked up the kettle and poured boiling water into the mug, then set it back on the stove before she turned around and joined him at the bar.

"Wouldn't you rather be catching and cuffing thugs than be trapped in this safe house looking after me?"

An amused grin bowed his mouth, and his eyes narrowed as he watched her in an all-consuming sort of way.

She kept her gaze focused on the lines of his handsome face to avoid looking at his naked chest.

"Is that what you think? That you're preventing me from searching for Wendy Davis?" He cocked his head slightly, his voice low, sexy and laced with challenge. "What if I told you I'm beginning to believe you are pivotal to this case?"

She emotionally pulled back, frightened by the prospect. "I'd say you're wrong. I don't know what my role is, or why someone wants me dead, but to put me in the middle of it is…well, it's…." What was it? "Unconscionable."

"I'll rephrase it in clearer terms. You *are* the center of this case, or at least your perceived abilities are."

Fear needled her senses, pierced her psyche and drew her emotionally back into the fray. "Because I sketched the women in the crime scenes, my own included, that somehow puts me in the middle of everything? That's an uncomfortable place to be."

"Come here, let me show you something." He shuffled through the papers in front of him until he found the one he wanted, and picked it up. "You're a Beholder. A term you believe was coined by a voodoo sect called the Materia."

"Yes."

"I had the police's research department dig up everything they could find on the sect, and this is it." He fingered a couple of sheets of paper. "Paragraphs of information any school kid could find in the study of local history. I have even been advised by the research department to consult with someone in the local voodoo community, a Miss Marie, to get an account of the unwritten lore."

Curiosity pushed her around the bar and onto the stool next to him. "So you're beginning to believe in what I do?"

"I'm conflicted. I don't know what to think."

Disappointment chilled the air between them and she felt the temperature drop ten degrees. "Then how is any of this going to make sense to you? It's like wearing half your skin if you don't believe."

Why did she feel compelled to convince him her gift was real? It had always been a secret she was happy to conceal because it offered her immunity, but now she *had* to make him understand.

"I can prove it to you." She reached out and put her hand

on his forearm. "Please." The contact seared her fingertips and brought Royce around on his stool.

"Let me sketch a composite of the man who abducted your sister when you were little."

His brows pulled together, suggesting to her that he was at least considering her proposal.

Royce's pulse suddenly spiked, riveting his focus on Adelaide's lips. Who was he kidding? He wanted to kiss her again, needed to kiss her again. Desire flooded his insides and ebbed like a Mississippi River eddy, surging for release.

"Okay. I will give you one shot. After that I never want to hear it mentioned again."

Her eyes went wide. A smile parting her sensuous mouth, a move that drove his tongue into his cheek as he watched her slide off the stool and hurry into the bedroom for her sketch pad.

In search of a distraction, he slid off the stool and stepped into the kitchen, where he wrung her tea bag out against a spoon and set the mug on the bar.

Adelaide appeared with her sketch pad and a pencil in hand. "Come over here on the sofa and get comfortable." She patted the cushion next to her.

A growl stuck in his throat as he picked up the cup of hot tea and walked in to the small living area, where he set the steaming mug down on the coffee table before pushing back into the oversoft couch.

This was the last place he'd planned to be sitting, but a commitment was a commitment, and she wasn't going to stop asking until he cooperated.

"It's simple. I want you to relax and close your eyes."

A reasonable request, he decided as he slouched and put his head back.

"I want you to picture what you saw that night." Her voice was low and soothing, almost hypnotic. Maybe that was how she pulled off her trick in person, although he still wasn't sure how she'd come up with the accurate sketches of the women.

"Bring the image to life for me inside your mind."

A surge of emotion clobbered him from out of nowhere. He pulled in a deep breath as he tried to experience that night again, just the way he had as a terrified six-year-old.

In the background he heard Adelaide's pencil working on the paper. Her graphite strokes amplified in his eardrums. "It was dark, but we had a night-light plugged into the socket between our twin beds. I guess that's how I saw his face when he bent down and covered my sister's mouth with his hand. No hat, I can see his hair, or what there is of it. Dark. I don't see his eyes, they're shadowed." He worked the fuzzy image in his brain, grasped for more detail, but got nothing.

"What did his mouth look like? Were his lips thin, thick? Did they match, or was one fuller than the other?"

"I'm not sure. Wait." He tried to dial in a faint memory about the man's mouth, but he couldn't make it clear.

"Nothing. I'm not even sure I saw his lips, but his chin was squared off, and—"

"I'm finished," she said, a note of excitement in her airy voice.

His eyes flicked open, he rocked forward and sat up, satisfied he'd upheld his end of the bargain, but irritated by the fact that his guilt had been resurrected from the grave he'd buried it in and laid bare like an unprotected wound.

"This is the man who took Kimberly." She turned the drawing around and held it out to him.

A numbing sensation started behind his eyes, soaking, saturating, until it found its way inside his chest. His heart squeezed.

She'd captured the exact image, the clear twin to the fuzzy description he'd been carrying around in his head for twenty-nine years. He focused on the jagged scar descending from the right-hand corner of the man's mouth. It was a fact he fully remembered now, but a fact that had always eluded him. Until now.

Reaching out, he took the sketch pad, feeling its weight in his hands. It was real, solid, tangible.

This was no trick.

"His scar is an unusual physical characteristic. If he has a criminal record, you will probably be able to find him with an image search in the department database."

Royce felt the first solid breath of air immigrate into his lungs.

Adelaide Charboneau was the real deal.

Her claims were legitimate. She had a talent that defied logic. He let the definition merge into his vocabulary and his thinking. He stared at her, seeing her for the first time. Feeling how vulnerable and in danger she really was, based on the information he'd picked up today.

"Tell me you believe me now," she pleaded.

"I believe you." He put the sketch pad on the coffee table and reached for her.

She moved into his arms, leaned into him and tucked her head up under his chin as he encircled her in his arms.

The contact scorched him, burning through his body like lightning. He closed his eyes, letting the fire forge him while he held on to her.

Outside, the storm intensified, shedding rain against the window in a torrent now, and pounding a drumbeat on the roof.

Royce resisted the urge to tighten his grasp on her. To conceal her, hide her from whoever, or whatever wanted to harm her. Caution fleshed out the uneasy sensation in his bones. "Where is the gris-gris you got from your mother today?"

"On the nightstand."

"You need to keep it with you at all times. Put it in your pocket, put it on a chain around your neck, just keep it close."

She sat forward and turned to look at him. "What are you talking about?"

"How much do you know about the Materia and their Beholder?"

"I know the parameters of what a Beholder is capable of doing. Shedding light on the criminal deeds of others. The proof is in my abilities."

"That's it?" He resisted the urge to finger a dark curl lying against her shoulder. "That is as far as your understanding goes on the subject?"

"What else is there?"

Worried for her, he stood up and took her hand, pulling her to her feet before he let go. "The Materia sect may not have anything to do with voodoo. They first turned up in New Orleans in the mid-1800s. They were peaceful healers, taking care of people's aliments with herbs and natural remedies, but word spread through voodoo lore about the uncanny abilities manifest in their Beholders."

"And you've read these legends?"

"No."

"Then how do you know they're true?"

"I don't, but it explains what's going on. The sect was targeted and destroyed. Wiped out one by one through ritualistic murders, all preformed by voodoo practitioners to negate a Beholder's magic. To keep the Beholder from exposing the criminals in society and their crimes."

"Stop." Adelaide's hand went to her heart. "You're scaring me."

"Good. You need to be scared. If it helps protect you, then it's worthwhile. Come over here, I want to show you something." He headed for the bar and shuffled through the information, picking up the pertinent page he was looking for.

"Your gris-gris isn't a traditional voodoo blessing doll, it's a Materia protection doll."

Adelaide took the paper from him and stared down at the information, combating a wave of unease. Things were beginning to make sense.

The description of the crude doll matched the gris-gris on the nightstand in the bedroom. It had a faded blue ribbon tied around its waist to secure its muslin gown. The five-inch-long body was composed of heavy cloth, hand stitched together with thick thread.

"This describes the doll that was found with me in the church."

"Yes. But the main reason to keep it close is for its protective qualities. Anyone who believes the doll has the power to protect will be less likely to harm you if you have the doll in your possession."

"My birth mother knew I was a Beholder. She was trying to protect me?"

"And hide you. There's one additional piece of information in the puzzle. Only the females in the Materia sect carried the gift. It didn't make any sense to me, until now, but you were found dressed all in blue. You were thought to be a baby boy when the priest discovered you, and it wasn't until after Children's Services picked you up that they discovered you were a girl. My guess is, your mother wanted to delay the discovery of your gender for as long as possible. Even the newspaper reported a baby boy was abandoned. They printed a correction, but not until a week later, and buried on a back page in a couple of sentences."

"She was running for her life." She put the paper back on the bar. "And for mine."

"Probably."

Stepping close to Royce, she moved into his open arms.

"Get some rest. I'll be on the couch, and I'll see you in the morning. We'll head over to Tulane to talk to your old professor about the Songe mask we found at Clay Franklin's place."

She didn't move. She wanted to stay in the safety of his arms indefinitely.

Did he feel it, too? An unsatisfied longing growing between them?

Her heart rate ticked up, and his arms tightened around her for an instant before he released her, setting her back at arm's length.

She looked up into his face, seeing the turmoil raging inside him through his dark eyes, through the catch in his breath as he returned her gaze and pulled her against him again with a growing intensity that threatened to drown them both. But it was a storm she couldn't fight any longer.

Royce caved in, staring at her mouth, then back up into her green eyes, eyes that seemed to convey her need to touch, to be touched.

"Adelaide," he whispered as he lowered his mouth to hers and brushed her lips, encouraged by the willing way she kissed him back. He was hungry to taste her, entangle himself in the web of need binding him to her with uncontrollable urgency.

He deepened the kiss, parting her lips with his tongue as he teased a responsive moan from deep in her throat. Heat fanned out over his body, drilling and tapping him for an explosion he knew he wouldn't be able to contain. He wanted her. Moving his hand up, he cupped the back of her head, driving her against him. They were in the fast lane, headed for a crash. An instant of clarity rocked his senses, and he slammed on the brakes.

She was his to protect, not seduce.

He released her in a sudden jolt of physical control, even though his pulse was hammering inside his head, and he couldn't suck in nearly enough oxygen to calm his body. "I have a sworn duty to protect you, not—"

"Don't." She held up her hand, looking vulnerable with the

soft glow of arousal manifest on her cheeks in rosy patches. "I know the drill, let's leave it at that."

He nodded, swallowing hard as he watched her turn for the single bedroom in the small safe house, a room he wanted to follow her into.

He took a step forward.

The light over the bar went out, plunging the room into total darkness.

Royce froze midstride and got his bearings in the unfamiliar room. He turned his attention to the plate-glass window, looking for confirmation that the power outage was widespread, but the flicker of house lights through the trees on the next block over sparked a warning deep in his brain.

"I think I saw a couple of candles in the cupboard above the stove. Do you want me to get them?"

"No lights. I want you to go into the bedroom and lock the door, steer clear of the window. The place is a fortress, it's been reenforced, you'll be safe inside. I'll give you the all clear when I'm finished checking it out. Keep your cell phone handy."

Over the wind and rain, he listened for any sound of a full-on assault, but didn't hear anything. Still, he had to assume the outage wasn't caused by the storm.

"Okay." Her soft reply was followed by the sound of the bedroom door closing and the dead bolt sliding into place. It was a good sound. A safe sound. A sound that soothed his unease.

Royce ran his hand along the back of the sofa until he reached the end.

Turning to the left, he put a hand out in front of him, feeling for the bar. He found it, worked his way over the paperwork he had spread out and patted his gun where it lay at the end of the counter.

He pulled the Glock out of its holster, turned and stood still, assessing the various access points in the room. The main front door was reinforced. All the windows, save one, were high up in the walls and made of bulletproof glass.

That left the plate-glass window. It, too, was bulletproof, but it overlooked the backyard and a string of trees at the border that could easily conceal an intruder.

He focused his attention there, studying the wave of dark and light shadow distorted through the rain-obscured window.

Movement. He saw movement, a person darting across the lawn in the back of the house.

Royce dropped to the floor out of sight and pulled his cell phone off his belt. Punching in 911, he notified dispatch of the situation and requested backup.

A loud thump against the side of the house pulled his attention toward the kitchen. The windowless room seemed like the last place someone would try to gain access.

He came to his feet and raised his gun, moving in slow, precise steps into the kitchen, where he listened to the sound morph into a raking noise that ended with a thud on the roof over his head.

Tension took up the slack in the air and bunched the muscles between his shoulder blades.

Did the intruder know the house was impenetrable? What about the roof? No one had ever come in through the roof.

Wham! The first blow rocked his reality. He stumbled back against the bar and stared up at the ceiling.

Wham! Another punishing blow hammered into the roof, causing the pendant light over the bar to sway.

"Damn." They were hacking their way through the ceiling. He'd think it was brilliant, if it weren't so off the wall and dangerous.

"New Orleans Police," Royce bellowed. "Stop or I'll shoot."

Wham! Another chop followed the sound of wood succumbing to the force. They'd get inside if he didn't take action.

Royce raised his weapon and squeezed off two rounds.

The slugs tore through the plaster overhead and rained debris down on him where he stood in the middle of the kitchen floor.

He listened, feeling sweat erupt at the hairline on the back of his neck and tickle his skin.

Nothing but the slightest flurry of movement over the sound of rain on the roof.

Sucking in a breath, he backed out of the kitchen and headed for the bedroom, his eyes now fully adjusted in the darkness. He reached the door and rapped on it several times.

Nothing.

Caution ramped up his nerves. "Adelaide. Open the door."

The dead bolt turned, the door opened, and she stepped back. "I heard shots. What's going on?"

"Our location has been compromised. Someone tried to get in by chopping their way through the roof in the kitchen. I fired a couple of rounds, and it stopped."

"What are we going to do?"

He reached for her, discontent until he felt her upper arm in his grasp. "We're going to wait it out. Backup is en route. If we go outside, we could be ambushed. It's hard to say how many of them there are. We're safer in here."

Adelaide couldn't keep from focusing on the fear that lodged inside her with an icy grip that wouldn't relent.

They were being hunted by desperate people. People bent on destroying them by any means.

She pulled in a short breath and tried to relax, feeling the crude gris-gris doll she'd wrapped in a cloth handkerchief and tied around her ankle for safe keeping.

It had to be her imagination, but she could almost believe she felt warmth emanating from it.

"GOOD CALL, DETECTIVE." Officer Brooks stood next to Royce in the small living room of the safe house. "There's a hole that was dug through the first layer of the roof above the kitchen. Someone wanted in here pretty bad. But I didn't find evidence of anyone outside now. We'll stay posted outside until morning."

"Thanks, Brooks."

The officer left, and Royce stared up at the ring of rainwater beginning to drip from the saturated plaster of the kitchen ceiling, watching it fall and drop into the large pan he'd set on the floor to catch the water.

He glanced over at Adelaide where she sat on the sofa with her legs tucked up underneath her and her eyelids closed. It was two in the morning and he knew she was exhausted. He was, too.

"Hey," Royce said, moving to the sofa and pressing his hand on her shoulder.

Adelaide started, her eyes flicking open.

"We're staying until morning. Brooks and his partner are stationed outside. Get some sleep."

"Yeah, all right." She stood up and walked a crooked line into the bedroom.

Listening for the dead bolt to turn, he flopped onto the couch the instant he heard it engage.

He was dog-tired.

Royce pulled the sofa pillow under his head, adjusted it and closed his eyes, listening to the ping of rainwater on stainless steel.

THREE HOURS LATER THE obnoxious ring of his cell phone dragged him awake.

"Detective Beckett."

"What the hell happened there last night?" Danbury said, his gruff voice erasing the grogginess from Royce's brain.

Royce sat up. "Leaky roof."

"Are you both okay?"

"Never better." Royce stood up, heard the bedroom lock turn and watched Adelaide walk into the living room.

"I need you on a scene. Another woman has been found murdered. The body was placed just off Highway 45 near Bayou Segnette. We're congregating at the Segnette boat ramp."

Royce's heart sank. "Wendy Davis?"

"That's what the I.D. in the open wallet says. We're headed out there now. It's a mess, thanks to the storm. Gina and her team are en route."

Adelaide reached out and touched Royce's back. "Did they find her?" she whispered. "Is she alive?"

Royce shook his head, sending her emotions on a roller-coaster ride.

They were too late. Too late to save the young woman whose face she'd sketched only days ago.

"We'll get cleaned up and be on scene within the hour," Royce said, glancing over at her.

She swallowed hard, blinking back a blaze of tears that threatened to spill over.

How were they ever going to get in front of this runaway train?

Chapter Eight

Dawn broke through the hazy rain, but Royce hardly noticed as he stood on the crowded patch of boggy earth dotted with inland salt grass, and listened to the rain pelt his slicker.

The low-lying area served as overflow for Bayou Segnette, and it was now filling fast with the deluge from Tropical Storm Kandace, almost faster than the evidence team could work.

Adelaide stood next to him looking tired, wet and expressionless in a hooded plastic poncho he carried as a spare under the front seat of his car.

Refocusing his attention on the crime scene, he studied the path the killer would have had to take down the ultrasteep embankment from the highway above.

He stared at the line of press vehicles parked like vultures at the guardrail, waiting for any scrap of information that might come their way.

Turning back to the question of how the body had arrived at this spot, he realized it wasn't impossible to bring her down from the highway, but it was highly unlikely she'd been dragged. There were no scuff marks on her shoes, no damage to her clothing.

The killer, or killers, must have placed Wendy Davis's body in the overflow using a boat to transport her to the location. The main Outer Millaudon Canal was less than five hundred feet to the north, and intersected a narrow tributary that was fifty feet away and flooding to the east.

"Anything?" Adelaide asked, moving to his side.

"Nothing that looks suspicious. He probably brought her here by skiff, or a small flat-bottom fishing boat. He'd have been seen if he'd used the highway."

A piercing whistle cut through the sound of the rain on his slicker, and he turned around, guiding Adelaide back to where Wendy Davis lay on the ground in a ring of mostly dissolved salt. Eyes wide open, hair spread out around her face, open wallet next to her, and the index finger of her right hand pointing, just like Missy Stuart.

He knew it was the last place Adelaide wanted to be.

Chief Danbury stood at the head of the small group of police and CSI, wearing the same dark blue slicker plus the title Incident Commander on the front and back in bold white letters. "Listen up, people. The water is coming up fast, and this dirt will be covered within the hour. The coroner is en route to remove the body. I want everyone to clear the area immediately, but beware, this flooding will push some nasty creatures our way. Stay alert for anything with teeth. Alligators. Snakes. You know the drill."

Everyone nodded, and the group broke open, some moving to the boats docked on the sliver of land for a ride to higher ground.

Gina Gantz and her team continued to process the body and scour for evidence that would soon be covered by water and lost forever.

Royce saw Gina wave him over, and he caught hold of Adelaide, bringing her with him.

Gina pointed at Wendy Davis. "See her eyes?"

He leaned closer, noticing that they weren't the same color. One was brown, the other light hazel. "Yeah."

"It's heterochromia, could be hereditary, or the result of disease or injury."

"Her missing person's report specified that her eyes were brown," Royce said.

"She probably wore a single brown contact lens," Gina said, making a notation on a soggy piece of paper attached to a clipboard. "We'll never find the lens out here."

Royce glanced around the terrain and had to agree. Something as minuscule as a contact lens could easily vanish or simply blend in with the bayou mud.

One by one the boats filled as personnel finished their assignment, and shoved off.

Only a single boat remained with a hooded, slicker-clad boatman huddled in the back next to the motor.

"Beckett."

Royce turned toward the chief. "Yeah."

"You two take the last boat. Gina and I will ride out with the body and the coroner."

Royce nodded, glad he could finally get Adelaide out of the wilds and back to civilization. "Thanks, Chief."

Danbury waved him off, and he steered Adelaide to the small aluminum boat. Grasping her upper arm, he helped her into the front, shoved off and climbed in, taking a seat next to her on the bench as he listened to the distinctive dragonfly putter of the nine-point-nine horsepower Evinrude.

The driver circled the boat in the water, revved up the motor and headed north toward its conflux with the Outer Millaudon Canal.

The abrupt turn threw Adelaide off center, and she put her hands down on the cross-bench to steady herself, watching the water smooth away from the bow of the boat and create rain-dotted ripples in its wake.

She glanced over at Royce, who seemed focused on the shoreline.

"Look at that." He pointed to a patch of gray-green marsh grass on the left-hand side of the boat.

"Look at what?" She strained to locate the specific object,

finally spotting what looked like a log bobbing in the water on the edge of the scum-crusted bank.

"Alligator," he said, leaning over to speak into her ear, over the hum of the engine. "Just waiting for his supper."

She knew bad things lived in the water. Things that could easily eat a full-grown adult if not given a wide berth and the respect they deserved.

A shudder vibrated through her, forcing her to look for danger wearing camouflage among the palmettos, marsh grasses and moss-dressed cypress trees standing knobby-kneed in the cloudy water, but the defensive tactic had little effect on the unease crawling through her body.

Searching the interior of the tiny boat, she focused on a canvas bag tucked in the front of the bow with the words *Emergency Kit* in red letters across the front of it.

She was out of her element among these creatures and the unforgiving environment. Just knowing help could be in that little bag calmed her somewhat.

In the distance she heard the putter of another boat, and looked up as the flat bottom passed, carrying the coroner and a boatman to the crime scene.

The tributary narrowed and brought them close to a cluster of Tupelo gum trees shagged with low-hanging moss.

Adelaide ducked to avoid being swept by it, but she couldn't avoid the trail of dripping water that splashed across her forehead and rolled down her face.

"Jeez." She reached up and mopped the water off with her hand before glancing over at Royce.

"Afraid you might get wet?" An amused smile spread on his lips, then faded slowly, taking her moment of pleasure with it.

He reached out and plucked something from her forehead, immediately cupping it in the palm of his left hand.

"Does it bite?" she asked, assuming the worst. Just her luck to wind up stung by some swamp spider who'd housed himself in the dangling moss and caught a ride on her head.

Royce's nerves thinned as he smoothed the perfectly round, brown object between his thumb and index finger. The manual examination confirmed his suspicions and solidified his concern. It was a single colored contact, the kind Wendy Davis wore to hide her heterochromia. The same kind that was missing from her right eye now.

This had to be the boat used to transport her to the patch of boggy soil where she'd died. How else could it have wound up on Adelaide's hand. It must have come from inside the boat.

Staring at the lay of the tributary, he gauged the distance to the shoreline as it widened into a sweeping turn, and fractured in several directions.

The moment of decision. Either the man at the helm was the killer, or he wasn't.

Adelaide sucked in a deep breath, feeling an oppressive sensation of dread sink into her bones.

Something was wrong. Something was horribly wrong. She glanced around, spotted a patch of iris she'd pegged as they'd motored into the tributary. She liked to know where she was, liked to be oriented.

Next to her on the bench, Royce brushed her leg with his right hand at the same time he opened his left one.

She stared at the clear brown object.

"Did you touch the body?" he asked in a voice so close to a whisper, she practically had to read his lips as she watched him speak.

"No." Looking back down at the flimsy object, she reached out and fingered it, making a tactile discovery. It was a soft contact lens.

"Where did you find it?"

"You brushed it onto your face with your hand. It came from somewhere in this boat."

She had touched the bench they were sitting on in order to steady herself and must have come in contact with it then. Now she understood the hush in his voice, the warning in his dark eyes.

The man operating the craft could be Wendy Davis's killer.

"It's evidence. I'll take it. I can keep it safe."

Tenuously she picked up the lens from the palm of his hand. Tension coiled around her insides. Evidence had to be preserved. If the lens were to dry out, they might lose it. She hesitated for a moment, then put it in her mouth, an action that seemed strange even to her, but her mother wore contacts, and saliva could be used to preserve it safely.

Using her tongue, she found the concave and forced it against the roof of her mouth, feeling it seal to her upper pallet.

"You ate it?" Royce whispered, agitation in his response.

"No. I'm making sure it's safe."

His eyes widened for an instant, and she watched him pop the buttons on his rain slicker and reach inside.

Royce locked his hand around the butt of his Glock and pulled it out of its holster.

"I want you to get down when the action starts." He didn't want her to get hurt.

"Okay."

Behind him he heard the Evinrude's rpm tick up. Had the driver turned on the governor?

Turning slowly, he caught sight of movement in his peripheral vision. He rocked forward off the bench seat, staying low as he pulled his pistol.

Crack! The boatman slammed an oar into the side of his head.

Royce took aim and squeezed off a round as a curtain

of darkness blackened his vision for an instant, but he was already listing hard to the left side of the boat.

A quick pull on the rudder by the boatman, whose face was buried in his rain hood, and his fate was sealed.

The craft jerked hard in the opposite direction of his momentum.

Royce launched over the side of the boat and slammed into the murky water, hearing only a note of Adelaide's scream before he sank below the surface.

He hit bottom with his feet and pushed hard, clawing for the top eight feet above, fighting against the drowning effect of his heavy slicker.

Air, he needed air. His gun was gone. Adelaide was gone.

He broke the surface choking and gasping as he scanned the water for the boat, spotting it in a sharp turn that kicked up a rooster tail less than fifty feet away.

Panic sucked him back down under the water as the boat roared over the top of his head.

He kicked to the surface, and watched in horror as Adelaide stood up and lunged for the boatman.

The impact sent the boat on a kamikaze path toward the shore that ended in a blitz of white water as the crash was averted and the boat came around again headed straight for him.

Where in the hell was Adelaide?

Panic clutched his body as he scanned the water for her. At the last second, he pulled a breath into his lungs and dove under.

Something splashed down ten feet in front of him, but he couldn't see in the murky water. He floated to the top, eyeing a commotion in the water.

Adelaide swam as hard and as fast as she could, listening to the hum of the boat just over her right shoulder. She'd never been good in the water, never had a need to be until now.

Focus, she had to stay focused on Royce.

Something brushed her leg below the surface, sending a jolt of terror through her. She kept paddling, keeping her focus on Royce, who swam toward her with powerful strokes.

He stopped and pointed at a dense patch of cypress on her left. "Shore," he yelled. "Get to the shore."

Determination drove her forward, spurred by the hum of the boat as it looped around for another pass.

Sucking in a breath, she dove deep.

The craft sliced through the water above her head.

She kicked for the surface in a flurry of air bubbles, refocused and kept on paddling, stroking for the bank.

Something brushed her leg again.

Her arms were on fire, the muscles burning with fatigue as she ignored the confrontation she knew lay just under the water. It was a fight she couldn't possibly win.

She put her feet down beneath her and felt the bottom. Fighting for traction in the bayou mud, she grabbed an exposed cypress root and pulled herself up onto the bank.

Behind her in the water she heard a splash.

In her peripheral vision on the right, she watched an alligator make landfall three feet behind her.

Panic ignited adrenaline in her bloodstream.

She ran forward and darted to the left, hearing him hiss as his jaws opened and he scrambled forward on his short legs like a lizard.

Alligators were fast in a straightforward charge, but not side to side.

She zigzagged again, working to pull her feet out of the muck with each running step.

Setting her focus on a point forty feet into the cypress, she ran from tree to tree, until she couldn't hear the reptile chasing her anymore.

Hunching over, she rested her hands on her knees. Her

lungs burned and her heart threatened to hammer out of her chest, but she'd managed to escape certain death.

Cautiously, she leaned out from behind the tree and stared at the path she'd taken, spotting Royce dragging himself up out of the water onto the bank.

The alligator had turned back for the water, and now stood between them.

Where was the boatman? She listened, but couldn't hear anything over the torrential rain.

Reaching under her poncho and inside her blouse, she pulled out the emergency kit she'd managed to snag from the front of the craft just before she jumped overboard.

She opened it, staring at the single item she'd prayed would be inside when she took it.

Yanking the flare gun out, she released the safety, raised it straight over her head and pulled the trigger.

A single flare fired, whizzing high above the treetops, where it ignited and began its slow fall back to earth. Chief Danbury, Gina Gantz and the coroner were sure to see it and come to help.

She squeezed off a second round for good measure and stepped out from behind the cypress tree to do battle, making eye contact with Royce in the gloom.

Royce eased slowly to the right in an attempt to put some distance between himself and the angry momma alligator hissing at him.

He was in a bad place, and he knew it. He eyed her egg mound, made out of mud and vegetation and tucked around the knees of an ancient cypress.

"Hold up, Adelaide. She's guarding her nest." Relief washed over him when he saw her stop and step in behind a Tupelo gum for protection. The girl had moxie, he'd give her that, and a flare gun they could use as a weapon against the reptile if they had to.

"I'm going to come around to you. Stay put."

Behind him in the water he heard the Evinrude sputter and die, restart and accelerate.

The crazy boatman was coming in for another pass, but the immediate danger was staring him down right now, and he couldn't take his eyes off the gator for a second, or he risked a full-on charge at an incredible speed.

"Royce!" The sound of his name in Adelaide's shrill scream was a moment too late. The blinding pain caught him behind the knees and slammed him to the ground, pinning his legs under the bow of the aluminum boat.

In an instant it registered. The boatman had rammed him from behind.

Adelaide rushed forward, raised the flare gun, took aim at the man in the flat-bottom boat and pulled the trigger.

The flare hissed in a straight line of smoke and sparks and hit him square in the chest. He launched out the back of the boat into the water.

The alligator charged.

Royce covered his head with his arms, prepared for the inevitable attack.

The alligator plowed into the water next to the boat.

Stunned, Adelaide dropped the flare gun and ran for the boat, listening to the terrified screams of the boatman in the water as he tried to escape the alligator.

She covered the distance to Royce and slid to a stop, watching the gator and the boatman vanish below the surface of the water ten feet out.

Her stomach clenched. A wave of nausea pushing up her throat, she sucked in a breath and focused on Royce. "I'm going to push the boat back."

"Easy, my legs are trapped, and we need the boat to get out of here."

She put one hand on either side of the bow's point and leaned into it. The boat inched back from its wedged-in-the-mud position and went buoyant on the water.

Royce raised up onto his hands and knees, and sat back. "Nothing's broken, thanks to the muck. Get in the boat."

She nodded and slung her leg over the side of the hull. Royce climbed in, hurried to the rear, put the motor in Reverse, pulled the choke on and pushed the starter button. The Evinrude hummed to life. He cranked the throttle handle and the boat moved back away from the bank.

Seventy-five feet out into the water, and well out of the gator's path, he let off the gas and killed the engine.

"You did a good thing back there." He eased up off the boatman's seat and moved onto the bench next to her.

She turned a teary green gaze on him, and he put his arm around her shoulders, pulling her against him.

"He would have killed us both, you know that don't you?"

"Yes, but that was a horrible way to die."

He couldn't disagree, but he was thankful it wasn't them. He watched the alligator break the surface of the water and crawl onto shore next to her nest.

Somewhere in the bayou a motorboat engine revved, and he glanced around to see Chief Danbury, Gina Gantz, the coroner and their boatman cruise toward them and cut the power.

"Beckett, what the hell's going on? We saw the flares. Where's your boatman?"

Royce didn't release Adelaide. "He tried to kill us. Adelaide hit him with a flare and forced him into the water. A gator got him. We need a recovery team out here to drag for his body. It's here, between us and the shoreline."

Danbury reached inside his slicker and pulled out his handheld GPS unit. "I'll mark it and call in the dive team. Any idea who he is?" Danbury asked, staring at him from inside his hood.

"No, but we did find Wendy Davis's missing contact lens in this boat."

Adelaide brushed the lens off the roof of her mouth, onto the tip of her tongue.

"Good thinking," Gina said, already pulling a plastic evidence bag open.

Adelaide pinched it with her fingers, pulled it off the tip of her tongue, and flicked it into the bag.

Royce released her and moved into the boatman's seat.

An icy chill skittered over Adelaide's body, robbing her of the security she'd felt only moments ago next to Royce.

Glancing up, she stared at the densely wooded embankment in front of her, and felt the unsettling sensation of being watched. Her eyes picked up shadow and light, the movement of vegetation, all through the veil of rain, all conspiring against her ability to pick out anything specific.

"Get Miss Charboneau back to the station and file a report. I want detailed accounts from both of you."

Royce put the motor in Forward and fired up the Evinrude. "See you back at the station."

Adelaide tried to relax on the bench as the boat puttered forward. She was safe now. They were safe and alive.

She pulled in a deep breath and realized how cold she felt all over. She was partly responsible for a man's death. There was blood on her hands. Granted, it had been shed by an alligator, but it was still on her hands.

Chapter Nine

Royce crossed the briefing room feeling like a new man, without the layer of bayou sludge on his skin, and all of his limbs firmly attached.

He paused in front of the large whiteboard cluttered with the information to date on Missy Stuart and Wendy Davis.

A knot wound in his stomach as he scanned the photos of the crime scenes. They were ugly, but so was the fact that he had the mirror sketches upstairs locked in his desk drawer. He had an obligation to share that information. And soon.

"Care to speculate?" Detective Hicks asked from next to him.

"They're both posed in the same position. Both have the index finger of their right hand pointing in some direction. It's got to be a message of some kind. Can you calculate their GPS positioning and draw a line away from their bodies?"

"You should be running lead on this one."

He glanced over at Hicks. "I've got my hands full just trying to keep myself and Miss Charboneau breathing."

"I heard about your foray in the swamp this morning. Any idea who the crazy was driving the boat?"

"If the gator left anything, we'll get an ID."

"I'll plug the coordinates into the computer. Who knows, we could catch a break and find out what they're pointing to."

"Thanks." Royce listened to Hicks retreat and refocused

his attention on the board. Adelaide's only viable link to the dead women was the fact that she'd drawn the sketches beforehand. The same sketches her abductor had burned in an attempt to destroy her along with them, but was that enough to bring Danbury in on her secret? A secret just crazy enough to get her fired. He didn't want to do that.

Dread darkened his mood and left him feeling uneasy. He thought about her sitting upstairs in her office with an officer posted outside her door. She was safe for now and until there was a finite connection, he planned to wait it out. Besides, she didn't have any information that wasn't already in play.

Chief Danbury entered the room through the side door, followed by Officer Brooks and a couple of serious-looking guys in suits.

FBI?

Royce walked over, pulled out a chair at the table and sat down next to Detective Hicks, who was busy setting up his laptop. It was never good to surrender jurisdiction, but he could almost make a case for it now, if it helped nail the sick bastard before another girl died.

"Good afternoon," the chief said as the men all settled into their chairs on the opposite side of the table.

A collective response rumbled through the room.

"I've decided to bring in FBI Agent Craig Wilson and Special Agent John Petross, borrowed from their Behavioral Science division at Quantico. They're stationed at the bureau in Baton Rouge, and picked up on these two cases because they bear a strong likeness to an open case in their neck of the woods."

Royce's hearing went on alert, and he sat forward in his chair, feeling the first niggling of caution work through his system.

"I'll turn it over to them now, so they can brief you on the details." The chief opened his notepad and picked up his pen.

Special Agent Wilson flipped open a file folder and retrieved a stack of photographs. "Last July we encountered a series of murders in the Baton Rouge area." He sent the handful of pictures to the left around the table. "Five women were killed in the course of a month, then it stopped just like that. We believe the killer or killers left our area."

"Any leads on who might have committed the crimes?" Hicks asked as he shuffled through the photographs.

"We believe there was more than one perpetrator, but the connection between our case and yours is the posing of the bodies, the drug used to kill them and the circle of salt around them. We were never able to determine what its significance was, but there's some sort of ritual involved."

The hair on the back of Royce's neck bristled. "What about a common denominator among the women?"

"They were all around the same age, twentysomething, but all from various walks of life."

Hicks slid the photos to him and he picked them up, staring at each one in detail. Women with their hair spread out around their faces, women with their eyes wide open, and the index finger of their right hand pointed in an unknown direction, and the circle of salt around them.

"Did you ever GPS the alignment of the bodies to see if they intersected anywhere?"

"As a matter of fact, we did. Here's the resulting image." Agent Wilson shoved a map across the table to him.

Royce picked it up and stared at it, feeling his pulse rate climb like a rocket ship gearing up for the moon.

Dots to the north, south, east and west, and a single dot in the center where the lines intersected.

"Who was killed first?"

"Jenny McNicholes. We found her on the north side of town in a marsh. Vivian Chase was next on the south end of the line. The other two girls to the east and west, respectively, all of them placed at the same distance from the center."

"And the woman in the center?"

"Patricia Reed. We didn't put the murders together until after the fact. She was being stalked, and the MO was different."

"What did she do for a living?" Royce asked, trying to put together a puzzle of his own.

"Miss Reed was an art teacher at a local high school, and moonlighted for the police as a sketch artist. The local authorities assumed she'd upset a perpetrator she'd drawn, and that got her killed."

Another Beholder? Royce worked to suck in a breath, letting the information cement in his brain.

"We've got a similar situation here, Agent. Our sketch artist is being tormented." Chief Danbury stared across the table at Royce. "I put Detective Beckett in charge of securing her safety. He's done a hell of a job so far, but it hasn't been without its challenges."

"How did she die?" Royce asked, caution creeping into his thoughts. Forewarned was forearmed, and he'd use any means at his disposal to protect his Beholder. Even his own life if necessary.

"The police found her in the trunk of a car in another county. Her throat had been cut, and oddly enough she had a patch of hair missing from the back of her head. We never found it. The car was traced as stolen, and we didn't find a single piece of usable forensics. The case is still open with the Baton Rouge PD, and we're stumped about motive. None of the information regarding the intersecting lines of the crime scenes was ever released to the media."

The air sucked out of the room. Royce put his hands down on the table for stability. The sketch of Adelaide in the car trunk surfaced in the front of his mind, and he couldn't release it. History could repeat itself if he didn't stay vigilant.

"We'll exchange case details. Maybe there's something we missed." Agent Wilson fingered the crime-scene photographs and put them back into his folder. "Special Agent Petross is on assignment in Baton Rouge from our Behavioral Science unit at Quantico, Virginia. He put together a working profile. I'll turn the discussion over to him."

Royce pulled the small notebook out of his front shirt pocket along with a pen, wondering if anyone would notice him scribbling the phrase *nut job* on an entire page. It wasn't going to help the case, but it certainly described the type of individual or individuals capable of committing such heinous crimes.

Agent Petross picked up a stack of papers from in front of him, took one and passed the remainder around the table. "This is a synopsis of my profile in the Baton Rouge case. I found the similarities to your case are an exact mirror. Feel free to jump in with questions or comments as I go through it."

Royce stared down at the bullet points, realizing they did superimpose over their case. The information didn't sit well with him; it got up, and crawled down inside him.

"We don't believe the killings were perpetrated by a single individual. The logistics of the remote to semiremote crime scenes, the posing of the bodies, the intersection of the crime locations to a single fixed point all suggest some sort of ritualistic meaning to the murders. We suspect an organization, or cult—"

"What about a voodoo sect?" Royce glanced up at Agent Petross. "A sect that has strayed off traditional nonlethal practices, and taken to dark magic."

"We didn't rule that out, but if it's a sect that has gone rogue, they've never been documented."

Were they dealing with a voodoo sect that had yet to be identified? Or an amalgamation of sects, bent on destroying the Beholder? He liked the second option best.

"This mastermind has a God complex. Remember he's able to direct his followers to participate in murder—he's got a hell of a persuasive personality. He'll appear friendly to all those he comes in contact with, but it's a mask he wears so the world will accept him. He's controlling. He'll be in his mid- to late fifties, without a wife or children, but only because anyone who gets close to him is unable to deal with his overblown ego and strange behavior. That's where his followers come in. They see him as powerful, secretive, able to help them indulge their most primal desires."

Caution crept through Royce, caution and concern for Adelaide. It was all beginning to make sense in a sick sort of way. She was the Beholder at the center. The ultimate link and the ultimate target.

"That's what we're up against, folks, so don't hesitate to contact my office 24/7. The more we learn about these killings, the better our chances of tracking down the people who are responsible. We'll be here for the rest of the afternoon if you have questions, or better yet, answers."

Royce nudged Hicks and leaned toward him. "Can you do that cross-check on the two crime scenes, see if they line up?"

"Sure."

Royce watched Hicks pull up a map of the city and outlying areas. He entered the GPS coordinates for both murders and hit the calculate button. "They're in perfect alignment to one another."

"Look at that." Royce clamped his teeth together as he stared at the intersecting line between the scene on the north and the scene on the south. The straight line between them crossed over Adelaide's house on Saint Charles Avenue. Tension steeled his body, cranking down his muscles to the point of pain. There was only one question in his mind. One last definitive link between Adelaide and Patricia Reed. "Tell me, Agent Wilson, was Patricia Reed adopted?"

"Yes. We followed that information, but came up empty."

"She's his target, Hicks. Adelaide Charboneau is at the center of some wacko sect's obsession, and she's adopted."

"Have you got something, Beckett?" Chief Danbury moved around the table and leaned over to stare at Hicks's laptop screen.

"Beckett's right. The coordinates intersect across Miss Charboneau's house. And she has been the target of numerous attacks and attempts on her life."

"Use her house as a reference point, draw a line away from it, one due east, one due west." Royce swallowed and prayed they could catch a break.

Hicks typed in the information, and a single intersecting line appeared on the map.

"Use the existing distance coordinate we have from her home to the other scenes, and see where it ends up on the east and west."

Royce watched two more dots pop up on the screen. He leaned back in his chair, feeling his first wave of hope in days. "If they follow the pattern set in the Baton Rouge case, we could use it to catch them. The next victim will be found on the east side of the city. We have the coordinates. We'll stake it out. Catch them when they try to dump the body."

The room charged with palpable energy; it vibrated through him, making him almost giddy.

One by one the investigators milled around the laptop, staring at the image, contemplating a plan of action. Even Agents Wilson and Petross took a cursory look.

"What's out there, Hicks?" Danbury asked, returning to his chair on the opposite side of the table.

"Looks like it's just off General Meyer Avenue in Algiers. Let me pull up a topographical. There's a park at those coordinates. I'll get the exact address."

Royce looked up at the chief. "Have there been any reports of missing or abducted women?"

"None."

"Good. Maybe we can get in front of this thing before anyone else dies." But there was only one thing he wanted to get in front of right now, and she was upstairs. How much of this new information could he give her without scaring her even further?

"I'm beat, Chief. It's been a hell of a day."

"Go on, get out of here. Take Miss Charboneau to a nice supper. We booked you at the Sheraton on Canal for the night. The French Quarter safe house won't be ready until tomorrow." The chief reached into his front shirt pocket, pulled out a key and slid it across the table. "Don't trash this one, we're about out."

Royce suppressed a chuckle. Under all his gruffness, Chief Danbury had a heart of gold. "Thanks."

He stood up and pushed in his chair. "Hey, Hicks. Nice work."

"You, too." Hicks went back to staring at the computer screen and Royce headed upstairs, wanting to see Adelaide in the worst way. The discovery of the Baton Rouge case was something he hadn't seen coming.

How was Adelaide going to react when he told her she wasn't the only Beholder on the planet?

Realization charged up an old memory buried in the back of his mind, of a shoe box filled with disturbing pencil drawings sketched by his five-year-old adopted sister, Kimberly, twenty-nine years ago, of the box being scuttled away by his worried parents, and hidden in the attic. Was it possible she was a Beholder, too?

A month later, Kimberly was abducted, and found wandering in the French Quarter three days later, unharmed physically, but never the same girl. He knew that because he'd found the shoe box as a college freshman, looking for leftovers to furnish his dorm room.

Royce took the stairs, unnerved by the memory. He'd

have to follow up with a trip out to his parents' house for confirmation that the box still existed.

He made the landing and walked down the corridor to Adelaide's office, where the uniformed officer nodded and stepped aside. Royce knocked on the door.

"Come in."

Pushing it open, he was hit by the overwhelming smell of peppermint.

"Hey." She looked up at him from over the top of a sketch pad and smiled.

Royce closed the door and pulled up a chair across from her, glancing at the candle in the middle of the table. "So this is how you kick back?"

"Yeah. You'd be doing yourself a favor if you inhaled a bit more relaxing peppermint into your lungs, too. After this morning's near-death experience in the bayou, you could use some R & R."

"What are you working on?"

"A little something for you."

"Oh, yeah?" His curiosity bubbled up. "Can I see it?"

"You already have, sort of." She put down her pencil and tore off the sheet. "I figured that I'd try to make him older, get him closer to what he might look like now."

She handed the sheet across the table to him. "I'll help you comb through mug books if you'd like."

Royce stared at the drawing, at the face of the man he remembered from Kimberly's abduction. "Thanks. I might take you up on the offer."

He casually put the sketch down on the table, but his hand trembled as he pulled it back. "There's been a new development in the case."

Her eyes widened and she leaned forward. "Tell me…I mean, if you can. I know I'm not a detective, but I do work for this department."

"Our two victims aren't the only ones in the state."

Adelaide frowned, her eyes narrowing. "That's bad."

"Last year in Baton Rouge four women were killed, same posed right arm, hand and finger. Same cause of death, and all ringed in salt. The FBI worked the case and came up with some interesting conclusions."

"Same guy?" Her features tightened.

"Same group. They believe it's not the work of a single individual. But there's more." He trained his gaze on her.

"A fifth victim. A victim they were able to put geographically in the center of the murders. Based on her personal information, I believe she could have been a Beholder. She was adopted, Adelaide, just like you."

Her gaze riveted on his, her skin going colorless under the overhead light. "Another Beholder? I never considered there might be others out there like me."

He stretched his hand across the table to her. She took it without hesitation.

"It looks like it takes some doing for a Beholder to survive the inquisition and subsequent slaughter."

Her observation made sense to him. Hiding them out in the open. Visible, but invisible. *It was brilliant.* "That's why your mother dressed you all in blue. She knew she had to protect you, give you a fighting chance." He squeezed her hand, watching her eyes go misty like fog rolling in off the ocean.

Reaching up with his other hand, he cupped her cheek, feeling the softness of her skin against his palm. In a hypnotic gaze he was helpless to break, he studied the intricacies of her face, of the easy way her lips bowed in a sweet smile.

He wanted to reach across the table and pull her against him. Only the edge of the tabletop thrust against his solar plexus made him pull back.

He was her protector; he needed to act like one.

Royce reluctantly broke his hold on her. "What time do we get in to see the professor?"

"I couldn't get an appointment until tomorrow morning, after his faculty meeting. We're seeing him at ten."

"Good, then we've got time to run over to Spells-4-U for a visit with Miss Marie."

"Spells-4-U?"

"That's what it's called. She's a department source, and may have information we can use about voodoo tactics."

"Hmm. Okay, let's go."

He pushed his chair back and picked up the sketch she'd done for him. The man had aged, but the distinctive scar on his lip would always be the same.

Adelaide put the lid on the candle jar to extinguish the flame, and came around the table to where he stood at the door studying the drawing.

"Since there's no statute of limitations on kidnapping, I want to put his image into my computer program. Maybe we can get a hit."

"Maybe." He pulled open the door and followed her out into the corridor, almost running into Gina in the process.

"Hey," she said, glancing between the two of them. "We got lucky and found enough of the boat driver, after a grid search, that we were able to get a name, and a rap sheet." She handed the file to Royce.

"Mr. Matthew Pournelle was some kind of bad."

"That good?"

"In and out of prison over the last ten years. Robbery, assault, drugs. I'd say it's a good thing that gator was there to take care of him for you guys."

Royce smiled and glanced over at Adelaide, who didn't appear to share in the humor the opinion generated between the two of them. But then she'd witnessed the man being pulled underwater to his death.

"The contact lens you found had manufacturing information on it, and we were able to trace it back to Wendy Davis. Thanks for saving it, Adelaide."

"You're welcome, but it was comical to watch Royce believe for an instant that I'd actually eaten it."

Gina chuckled, turned and walked down the hall slightly ahead of them.

"How is that momma alligator, anyway?" Royce asked.

"Still guarding her nest, and probably glad we left her bayou before her babies busted out of their shells."

"Would you like to speak with the department's counselor, Adelaide?" He cast her a sideways glance before refocusing on the elevator doors at the end of the hallway. "It's routine when you witness a tragedy. The department has someone on staff for debriefing."

"I'm fine, Royce. I was just thinking that Matthew Pournelle would have gladly watched us being turned into gator food. It's poetic justice if you ask me. He got as good as he was willing to give."

They bunched up at the elevator, and Gina pushed the down button. "It's worrisome that every thug in this case has a lengthy criminal history, Royce. Both Clay Franklin and Matthew Pournelle showed an escalating propensity for violence. If they weren't dead, I'd believe they could commit murder the next time around."

Royce listened to the elevator doors slide open and followed the women into the cubicle, dissecting Gina's observation about Franklin and Pournelle. Both men had attempted to harm Adelaide, in somewhat different ways, but harm her nonetheless.

What if they were looking at it all wrong? What if her attempted abduction and the murdered women were linked by more than the fact that she'd drawn their death scenes? A knot formed in his stomach as the elevator chimed and the doors opened on the detective unit.

"Thanks, Gina." Royce pressed his hand into the small of Adelaide's back and steered her toward his desk in the corner as Gina broke off for the lab.

Excitement frayed his nerves and drove a series of maligned thoughts together inside his head.

"This will only take a minute. I want to run a comparison between Franklin and Pournelle's known associates. I bet we find they have a lot in common."

"Okay. But how does that help? They were both creeps, thereby proving the old adage 'birds of a feather flock together.'"

"Exactly. And among that list of scumbags could be the thug who kicked down your door and dragged you out of your house, the one who set the place on fire around you, and put Officer Tansy in the hospital, the one who took potshots at us out in Destrehan and the one who tried to hack his way into the safe house."

"A criminal network?"

"More than that, Adelaide." He put Pournelle's file and the sketch in his hand on the desk and slid an extra chair over for her.

"It's an organized hunting party, willing to do just about anything to get what they want. Find them, link them and you'll find the ringleader."

He resisted the urge to reach out for her, to hide her away somewhere safe until the danger had passed and he'd connected every dot. "The mastermind directing this gang of deviants is behind the murders, here and in Baton Rouge. He's one and the same. He destroys Beholders because he believes in their magic."

Royce watched her swallow and felt the blood turn cold in his veins. They were up against evil. Unreasonable evil that fed on people's darkest desires. He reached out this time and touched her cheek with his fingertips, feeling the contact jolt his insides.

"He's a hunter, Adelaide. And he has been hunting you since the day you were born. We need to visit Miss Marie to find out what we're up against."

ROYCE'S THOUGHTS WERE HEAVY as he escorted Adelaide along Bourbon Street in the late-afternoon sunshine that had chased Tropical Storm Kandace well to the east.

He'd dressed down in jeans and a T-shirt at Megan Lorry's suggestion. She'd convinced him that information would flow more freely if he didn't look like a cop when he spoke to the shop owner about all things voodoo.

"What's this place called again?" Adelaide asked.

"Spells-4-U, Voodoo Magic and More. It should be right here." Royce glanced up at the gaudy purple sign suspended from the overhang twenty feet in front of them.

"There it is. I never thought I've have to go into a place like this to work a case."

She glanced over at him. "Neither did I, and I suppose you think I frequent them?"

"No. I've developed the highest regard for what you do. It's not a parlor trick. It's the real deal. You're the real deal."

"Thanks." She grinned.

"We have strict instructions to play it cool. The department's source is adamant about keeping her anonymity."

He reached out and took her hand. "How's this for cool?"

"A couple out for a stroll in the French Quarter on a sultry afternoon? I like it."

"Good, because we're supposed to be here for a voodoo blessing on our upcoming nuptials." He pushed open the door to the little shop and they stepped inside.

The earthy aroma of patchouli incense overpowered Adelaide's senses as she scanned the interior of the store. A couple of patrons milled around a candle display that stood six feet tall, and contained candles in every color she could name, and some she couldn't. Another display dangled with charms and cloth bags she assumed could be filled with powders, potions and herbs.

A young woman in a flowing skirt and a tight white blouse

knotted above her exposed belly button moved toward them. She stopped several feet away and stepped back.

"Can I help you?" she asked.

"We're here to see Miss Marie. We have an appointment for a marriage blessing."

"Oh, yes. I can see it in your auras. You two are meant to be joined. She is upstairs." The girl gestured to a stairwell in the back of the store and turned to help a customer with a handful of candles, casting a quick glance over her shoulder at the two of them before she turned completely away.

Royce raised his eyebrows and led Adelaide toward the stairs. This place gave him the creeps.

Pushing apart the bead curtain, he stared up the narrow stairwell and pressed through. They made the landing and stepped into a narrow room, painted the same hideous shade of purple as the sign outside.

A frail-looking old woman sat behind a small round table. She glanced up as they entered.

"Come. I've been expecting you."

Royce escorted Adelaide to the table, pulled out a chair for her and sat down in the one next to her.

"Miss Marie, we need your help."

The elderly woman looked back and forth between the two of them. "Ah, Miss Lorry sent you?"

"Yes."

"Then how may I help you?"

"Adelaide—" he gestured to her with a nod of his head "—is a Beholder. She's in the process of exposing someone who is killing young women. The murders are ritualistic in nature, and the victims are found posed and circled in a ring of salt. We believe the crimes are being committed by someone with a knowledge of voodoo."

"The salt represents bad luck, and it is being used to direct that bad luck onto someone else."

The victim's pointing finger?

"Has he taken anything from you, Adelaide? A trinket, a personal item, perhaps a lock of your hair?"

Adelaide felt an unsettling sensation move over her body. "A piece of my hair. He cut off a piece of my hair." She fingered the exact spot where the chunk was missing. Cut off by the man who'd attempted to take her the night Royce rescued her.

Miss Marie leaned forward. "Guard yourself well, child. Your white magic is powerful for good, your aura is obscured by it, but he can weaken you by possessing your hair, and the circle of salt can bring you bad luck. The circle of death he is creating around you could consume you, and he will destroy you if he has the chance. Do you have the protection doll of a true Beholder?"

"Yes."

"Keep it close, but keep your Protector closer."

"My Protector?"

She gestured with a hand, palm up. "He is your Protector, Adelaide. Your soul mate. It is his purpose, as dictated by the events of his life. The white light is strong around you both. But be warned, those who practice dark magic will try to separate you by killing him. That is all I can tell you."

It was enough, Royce decided as he stood up, dug into his pocket and pulled out a fifty-dollar bill.

"Thank you for your help." He held out the money, but she held up her hand.

"I cannot take it. You asked for my help, and I've freely given it to you. You know the way out."

Royce took hold of Adelaide's hand, headed for the stairs and escaped. He didn't want to admit it, but somewhere inside him, the old woman's words were resonating.

Every attempt that he believed had been directed at Adelaide had been meant for him.

Chapter Ten

Adelaide stared out the car window at the shadows that stretched across the sidewalk at the corner of Canal and Royal, where they sat waiting for the traffic light to change.

The sun and heat had managed to wring the rain-soaked city out, but even the presence of sunshine did little to burn through the layer of foreboding that had settled over her.

She ran her thumb over the gris-gris doll cupped in the palm of her left hand. "Do you think my birth mother could still be out there somewhere?"

Royce shot her a quick glance. "Anything's possible."

"Can you look through old police files from around the time I was abandoned?" Her throat closed, and the pressure of the emotion in her heart forced tears into her eyes. "I need to rephrase that, considering all the new information that has come to light. Maybe, around the time she saved me."

"Yeah. I can look into it after we catch these guys and things settle down."

The light turned green.

Royce pulled through the intersection, crossed Canal Street onto Saint Charles Avenue and braked on the bumper of another car. The going was slow; remains of traffic from the morning commute bunched up in front of them.

He looked in his rearview mirror, studying the silver car trapped on the other side of the street. Paranoid? Yeah, he was becoming more paranoid with every passing incident, and Miss Marie's spooky rant about dark magic hadn't helped.

"What's your professor's name again?"

"Charles Bessette. He always claimed he could trace his French ancestors back to Louis the XVI, and maybe he can, who knows. What I do know is he was one of my favorite professors."

Traffic started to move, and Royce moved with it, taking an occasional look in the mirror at the car following them, at the man behind the wheel wearing a ball cap and sunglasses.

"Cultural anthropology is a deep and diverse subject. He's a hands-on kind of guy, always taking off on sabbatical to verify historical accounts with concrete facts."

She smiled for the first time since they'd left the station, and it helped to ease the worry lacing through his veins.

"Looks like they're working on your house." Royce slowed a bit as they passed her home, its facade still marred by a strip of crime-scene tape looped around the impressive columns of the front porch. A couple of workmen were busy shuttling equipment inside, and a box truck with a huge paintbrush logo on the side was parked at the curb.

"My mother is overseeing the cleanup and restoration. It should be ready to move back into in a month or so."

In a month or so? Where would he be at that point in time? For some reason he couldn't picture anything beyond this moment, and that bothered him.

"Tulane is a big place. How do I get where I'm going?"

"Take Newcomb Boulevard to Freret Street. It's on the corner of Freret and Audubon."

Glancing into the rearview mirror, he made a decision and turned right onto the next street. Accelerating rapidly, he braked at the next intersection on the residential street and hung a left, watching as the silver car made the corner a block behind him.

"We're being followed again."

"What do they want?"

"You." At least that was what it had always been the times before. Someone wanted her in the worst possible way, and they were willing to kill him to get to her. But he wasn't going to let that happen.

Taking a hard right into a narrow alley, Royce zipped to the end and turned right again, easing out to see the silver car disappear around the corner in the opposite direction. He pulled out and drove back to Saint Charles and nosed back into traffic.

"I'm pretty sure I lost him, but keep an eye out."

"Okay."

Ten minutes later, he eased the car up next to the curb in front of the Anthropology Annex, an old two-story house conversion painted a shade of muddy white that reminded him of dust.

"This is it," she said. Reaching for the handle, she opened the door and climbed out of the car.

Royce leaned down, pulled the trunk opener and climbed out, stepping around to the open compartment for the Songe mask he'd tossed inside to keep from having to look at it. The damn thing gave him the heebie-jeebies. Had since the day they picked it up off the floor in Clay Franklin's house.

He leaned into the trunk and picked up the evidence bag and the manila envelope next to it. Pulling back, he closed the trunk and turned to stare down the street behind him, feeling the air sag with tension, but the street was clear save a handful of parked cars.

There was that paranoia thing again, but he couldn't let it take over and obscure his reasoning.

He stepped up onto the sidewalk and pressed his hand against Adelaide's back as they climbed the steps and entered the building.

A receptionist looked up from her spot behind a low counter. "Can I help you?"

"We have an appointment with Professor Charles Bessette."

"Go on up. He's on the second floor in room 200."

"Thanks." They climbed the stairs to the second floor and walked down the narrow hallway until they found room 200. A brass plaque on the door showed them they'd arrived at the right place.

Adelaide knocked.

"Come in."

She turned the knob and entered the office with Royce behind her.

Professor Bessette sat behind a large desk, staring at a computer monitor. He looked up at her from over a pair of wire-rimmed glasses and smiled. "Adelaide Charboneau. It is so good to see you again."

"Thank you, Professor Bessette. I wasn't sure you would remember me when I called for an appointment."

"Yes, well, I will admit, I wasn't sure who you were then, but the moment I saw your face I remembered you from my class last year." The professor stood up and looked at Royce.

"Detective Royce Beckett, New Orleans PD." He reached out and shook the professor's hand.

"Please sit down. I understand you have an artifact you would like me to examine?"

"Yes." Royce broke the seal on the evidence bag and pulled out the plastic bag inside containing the two halves of the mask. "We'd like your expert opinion on this Songe." He handed the bag across the table to the professor, who immediately began to open it.

"I'm sorry, sir, it's evidence. It has to remain sealed."

"I understand." He put the bag on the desk in front of

him and turned on his desk lamp, aiming its beam onto the mask. "It is most certainly a replica, and a poor-quality one at that." Pressing the plastic taut over the gruesome features, he studied it. "You could easily pick something like this up from a street vendor in the Quarter during Mardi Gras, or perhaps any time of year."

Royce opened the envelope and pulled out the drawing Adelaide had sketched at the hospital. The mask of the man who'd tried to kill Officer Tansy. "What about this one, can you tell us anything about it?"

He handed it across the desk to the professor, and saw him blanch as he studied the sketch.

"Oh dear. This one is quite a different matter."

"What do you mean?" Royce leaned forward, his interest piqued.

"Do you have this mask in your possession?" Bessette asked, his face contorted by a frown.

"No, sir."

"Good. You would not want to touch this one in the flesh. It looks like an authentic voodoo Songe judging by the language reliefs cut into the wood under the eye slits. It was used by the Susu voodoo sect in the early 1800s, and based on its high ridge crest, its black magic is very powerful. It was only handled and worn by the high priest in ceremonies of vengeance and retaliation."

"Retaliation for what?" Royce asked, hunching up one shoulder as a chill crept across the back of his skull. He could almost imagine that Professor Bessette believed in the nonsense he was telling them by the intensity in his voice.

"I do not know. The documentation is limited to a single manuscript from the early Susu."

"How would someone go about getting a mask like this?"

"It is highly unlikely that they could. In fact, the last one

I tracked sold at auction thirty-four years ago for over a hundred thousand. You see, they are carved out of soft wood, so naturally if not preserved properly they will succumb to time and the elements."

"Thank you for your help." Royce reached out, taking the two-bit mask and the sketch the professor handed back to him. He put the mask into the paper evidence bag and slipped the sketch into the envelope. He didn't know a single thug who had that kind of money who'd be willing to drop it on a wooden mask so he could wear it in the commission of a crime. He glanced over at Adelaide, who was focused on the professor.

"There's another artifact, Professor Bessette. If you wouldn't mind taking a look at it." Adelaide squeezed her gris-gris doll in her hand and reached out across the desk. "This belongs to me, but I don't know much about it. Maybe you can take a look." She opened her fingers, exposing the doll in her palm.

"Yes, well, it looks like a traditional gris-gris, used as a voodoo blessing. They are commonplace within many of the local sects. That, too, could be obtained at a local shop in the Quarter."

The professor's dismissive tone cut deep. She pulled the doll back. "Wouldn't you like to examine it?"

"Certainly, and you are welcome to leave it here with me if you like. Perhaps next week I could take a moment for a closer look. You could return for it then."

She closed her fingers around the doll, and instantly felt better. "No, thanks. I'll just keep it. I know enough about it to be satisfied."

"Have I offended you, Adelaide?"

"I just thought it was more unique than that."

"Perhaps it is. Please leave it with me. I promise I will give it a thorough vetting."

"That's okay. I think I'll hang on to it."

"Very well." The professor dipped his chin and stared at her over the rim of his glasses. "I hope I have been helpful to you both, but I really must leave, I have a lunch engagement in an hour. I will walk you out."

Royce stood up and grasped Adelaide's elbow as she rose out of her seat. He knew her feelings were raw, roughed up by the professor's dismissal of her gris-gris as commonplace, when he himself knew otherwise. To Adelaide it was priceless. More than cloth and old thread, it was her only link to her birth mother.

They left the office and headed down the stairs, with the professor right behind them. They stopped at the reception desk.

"If you wish to reconsider leaving the gris-gris just give me a call and drop it by."

"Thank you, Professor." Royce shook his hand again. "But she's rather attached to it."

The professor nodded and turned to Adelaide. "So nice to see you again, dear."

"You, too."

Royce guided her to the front door. He pulled it open and they stepped out onto the landing. He closed it behind them and took a moment to survey the street before moving them down the steps.

"I'm glad you didn't leave the doll with him."

"Me, too, but frankly I don't believe I could have, especially in light of what Miss Marie said."

Royce pulled the car keys from his pocket and popped the door locks, then the trunk lid. "It's irreplaceable. That's reason enough to hang on to it, and besides, it's infused with white magic."

She gave him a weak smile and climbed into the passenger

seat. He went around to the rear of the car and leaned in, about to put the envelope and evidence bag inside.

A streak of silver materialized in his peripheral vision on the left.

The roar of an over-revved car engine cut the air and pulled his head around. In slow motion he watched the silver car that followed them from the station race straight for him.

He dove for the curb and hit the sidewalk on his belly, dropping the items still in his hands. The air was forced from his lungs and he fought to pull it back in, just as the car slammed into the rear of his sedan.

Shattering glass rained down on him. *"Adelaide."*

He rolled over, sat up and pulled his weapon.

The driver put the car in Reverse and gunned it backward.

Releasing the safety, Royce squeezed off two rounds into the car's radiator, hoping like crazy he could stop the vehicle before the man in the ball cap and sunglasses took aim at them again.

He scrambled to his feet just as Adelaide scrambled out of the passenger seat onto the sidewalk.

The driver popped the car into Drive and shot forward.

Royce grabbed Adelaide from where she stood transfixed, watching the horror unfold, and hurried her toward the safety of the anthropology building.

Professor Bessette rushed down the front steps toward them.

"We have called the police," he said, his dark eyes going wide behind his wire-rimmed glasses.

"Adelaide?" He studied her as he came toward them, and flinched as the car sideswiped the sedan with a loud crunch, and the subsequent nails-on-the-chalkboard scrape down the entire length of the vehicle.

The silver car roared away, dragging the bumper with it

as it barreled down the street, took a left onto Audubon and disappeared.

Royce slowed their progress across the tiny yard and stopped next to Professor Bessette.

"It looks like a terrible hit-and-run. It is not the first time this has happened on this narrow street." The professor studied them over the rim of his glasses. "Come inside. The police are on their way. I had my secretary phone 911 the instant he ran into your car the first time."

"We appreciate that."

Adelaide sobered, letting the nerve-racking seconds that had preceded this moment catch up with her traumatized thought processes.

One second Royce had been stowing the Songe mask in the trunk, and the next he was diving for the sidewalk. He'd just come close to being killed, and that knowledge sparked real fear deep down inside her. It stayed there, wrapping around her bones as he released her and darted back to the sidewalk to pick up the bag with the Songe mask inside, and the envelope containing the sketch. He put them in the backseat of the car and turned around.

She watched him walk toward her, seeing the confidence in his stride, shoulders back, head up, while she had to work just to still her wobbly knees.

There was something about him that spoke to her senses on a gut level she couldn't quite grasp, and looking at him always churned up an insatiable need inside her. She glanced away, feeling the sting of heat ignite on her cheeks in hot little patches.

"I have got to leave." The professor touched her arm. "You will be okay?"

"Yes, thank you." She watched him walk up the steps and go back inside the building before she refocused on Royce.

"That maniac almost killed you."

"It'll take more than that to do the job. He followed us from the station and waited for us to come out. I fired two slugs into the radiator of his car. He won't get far." Royce opened his arms to her.

The sound of sirens in the distance filled the air, and she gladly stepped into the circle of his embrace. It was a sound they'd heard too often together.

She closed her eyes and tried to reconcile her scattered emotions with the man holding her. It all added up. He added up.

Royce smoothed his hand across Adelaide's head, feeling the silky texture of her hair under his palm. She shivered, and he pressed her tighter into his chest, staring over her head as a black Mercedes with the professor behind the wheel pulled through the driveway from the parking lot behind the building. Its clattering motor reminded him of a truck on the freeway. You didn't see many diesels around. He watched it pull out into the street and drive away, leaving a trail of dark smoke hanging in the humidity well after it was out of sight.

He sucked in a couple of breaths, remembering how much he liked the smell of burning diesel.

The information the professor had given them about the masks had only given him cause for worry. Not only were there thugs hiding behind them, but he wondered if they believed in the black magic surrounding them. There was nothing worse than superstition to erode common sense.

This case had it in spades. It was unpredictable and elusive. It was like squeezing jelly. It added an entire dimension that couldn't be controlled.

A black-and-white squad car rolled up on scene with its lights flashing.

Royce released Adelaide and prepared to give a statement to the officer and get them a ride back to the station after a tow truck hauled away the damaged car. But one unanswered question burned in the back of his mind.

How was it the thugs always seemed to know where to find them, even after he'd given them the slip?

ADELAIDE SPOONED ANOTHER BITE of fried rice into her mouth from out of the Chinese take-out container and looked across the desk at Royce, who nimbly raised chopsticks to his mouth loaded with noodles.

"You do this a lot, don't you?"

He grinned and ladled them in, sucking the tail of the last one through his lips. "Comes with the territory. Good food, bad hours, a mediocre life."

"You don't mean that last part, do you?"

A far-away look stole the humor from his summation, and he blinked a couple of times before digging in again. "Would it be significant to you if I did?"

"Yes, as a matter fact it would."

"Why? Give me one single reason to hope for something more than just so-so."

She could feel her cheeks warm. She'd managed to jump off the philosophical diving board smack into the deep end of the private pool. "How about finding love…and having a family?"

He chewed his next bite as he studied her, his dark-eyed gaze exploring her face. It was a tactic that left her breathless, and tiny jolts of nervous energy pulsed along her spine. Still, she wanted him to answer the question in the worst sort of way.

"Hmm. I get it. This is really about babies. Babies and a woman's ever-ticking biological clock, the one that makes Big Ben look like a cheap timepiece."

She wanted to wipe the smirk off his handsome face with

her lips, but she smiled at him instead and spooned up another bite of rice. "Seriously." She ate it, watching him watch her.

"Okay. I'll humor you. How about this. Being alone is slow hell."

She didn't disagree. "It is. Watching your life pass you by with no one to share in its ups and downs could be considered hell by some. So yeah."

Royce set his food container on the desk and rocked forward, feeling uncomfortable with the subject being batted back and forth between them. It hit too close to home for him. Too close to the things he wanted in his mediocre life. A wife, a home and babies, lots of babies.

"Come on, let's get out of here. We're going to have to catch a ride with a black-and-white unit. I have a trick to make sure we're not followed to the safe house tonight."

He was glad when she nodded, dropped her plastic spoon into the empty take-out box and put it in the trash next to his desk. He tossed his carton, too, and escorted her to the elevator, feeling tension in the air between them as it pressed down on him, making him wish he was better at the sappy stuff.

The doors slid open and he came face-to-face with Patrolman Stevens. "Detective Beckett."

"Stevens. What's up?"

"It's Officer Tansy."

The doors started to close. Royce put his hand out and stopped them, waiting until Adelaide had stepped across the threshold, then followed her in, watching the doors close. "Did he come out of the coma?"

"He died half an hour ago. The call just came in."

Royce reached out and grasped the railing, feeling the elevator sink along with his stomach. Another casualty of the low-life thugs wreaking havoc every chance they got as of late. "I'm sorry to hear that. Does he have a family?"

"Yeah, a wife and a couple of kids."

Adelaide reached out and put her hand on his arm, sending a jolt of heat into his body where the contact was made.

"If there's anything I can do, let me know."

"Just get the bastard who did it." Stevens straightened, blinking hard to conceal his emotions.

The elevator stopped on the ground floor, the doors opened and the patrolman stepped out, waiting for them to follow him.

"The patrol lieutenant said you need some sort of decoy to get to the safe house?"

"Yeah. We've been followed repeatedly. I need an officer to drive my car over and put it in the garage at shack 99, while Miss Charboneau and I go incognito in the backseat of a squad car, at least until we're away from the station."

"I think we can handle that. Let me get another officer." Stevens disappeared into the patrol division and materialized five minutes later with two more cops in tow.

"This is Montgomery Howard and Chance Jurkowski."

"Officers." Royce nodded and shook the men's hands, but he didn't like the way Montgomery Howard gave Adelaide a once-over and flashed her a broad smile. He had a reputation as the department's Casanova and it was showing right now.

"And you're Adelaide Charboneau, our illustrious sketch artist." He reached out and took her hand.

Irritation fired off in Royce's veins, but he extinguished it. He should be used to the reaction she stirred up in men's blood. Hell, he'd experienced its volatile effect more than once himself.

Adelaide watched Royce's shoulders pull back and his chin come up. If she didn't know better, she'd think he was jealous. "I'm not sure if that's good or bad, but it's nice to know my work is beneficial in helping you catch criminals." Pulling her hand back, she smiled up at the officer who stood much too close.

She stepped back and felt the reassuring grasp of Royce's hand on her elbow.

"Its been a trying day. I'd like to get Miss Charboneau to the safe house ASAP."

Officer Howard nodded. "We'll take your car. The place out in Metairie, shack 99?"

"Yeah." Royce fished in his pants pocket and pulled out the keys to his personal vehicle. He would have to wait until tomorrow to pull another fleet car, something that already had Chief Danbury tied in knots.

"The garage door opener is on the visor."

Officer Howard took the keys and left the station along with Officer Jurkowski, headed for the parking lot.

"We're all set. I'm in unit fifteen at the back of the lot. I'll see you in five after I grab a cup of coffee." Stevens handed Royce the keys and headed for the break room.

Royce steered Adelaide to the rear door of the station and glanced out into the half-empty lot. "Stay low and follow my lead."

"Okay."

He opened the door and stepped out into the thick night air. Notes of a jazz tune floated over from some nearby street. Hunching over, he took Adelaide's hand and pulled her along behind him as he slipped in next to a squad car.

Aiming his sights on car fifteen from the cover of the vehicle, he shuffled forward and darted in between the car's driver-side door and a barrier fence covered with ivy.

Sliding the key into the lock, he opened the door and hit the auto lock button, then closed it quietly and maneuvered to the back door.

He opened it and watched Adelaide crawl inside and slide

all the way over against the other side, careful to keep her head low. He followed her in and slouched in the seat.

"Do you have to do this sort of thing all the time?" she whispered in the darkness, which was riddled with light coming from tall fixtures spread around the perimeter of the parking lot.

"No. But if it proves my theory, and keeps you safe at the same time, I'd belly crawl across Lake Pontchartrain."

The sound of whistling stopped the instant Officer Stevens opened the car door and climbed inside.

Royce dropped the keys over the front seat.

Stevens fired up the engine and pulled out of the lot.

The sound of the police radio startled Adelaide, and she adjusted her uncomfortable position in the seat. "Unit fifteen, unit forty-two, go car-to-car transmission."

Stevens picked up the radio mic. "Unit forty-two, go ahead."

"Beckett was right, we've got a boogie on our tail, and we're en route to Metairie shack 99. We'll drive him around, show him the city and leave him in Metairie. You can pick us up at the corner convenience store."

"Copy that, unit forty-two. Have fun." He put the mic in its holder. "Did you catch that, Beckett?"

"Yeah. It's all clear, Adelaide." Royce pushed himself up in the seat and watched her do the same.

"Toulouse Street?"

"Yes. We'll walk over to the station in the a.m."

Adelaide was confused, but she kept it to herself, watching their progression down Royal Street to the corner of Toulouse, where Officer Stevens made a left-hand turn, drove a half block and stopped the car next to the curb.

"Thanks."

"No problem."

Royce opened the car door and helped her out of the patrol unit.

"What are we doing here? We never even left the French Quarter."

"It's safer that way. Come on." He led her into the alley and up a flight of fire-escape stairs that ended at a narrow door. Reaching into his pocket, he pulled out a single key and pushed it into the lock.

"What is this place?"

"A department safe house."

"But I thought the safe house was shack 99."

He pushed open the door, reached around the corner and flipped on the inside light, then pulled up the stairs, leaving them stranded on the landing thirty feet above the ground.

"Shack 99 is my place. I just hope it's still standing in the morning when the thugs figure out they've been duped."

Chapter Eleven

Adelaide stepped into the studio apartment and looked around.

"Home sweet home," Royce said from behind her as he closed the door and locked it. "The place was stocked this afternoon. There's food, and your belongings were brought over from the hotel. There's even a sketch pad for your drawing pleasure. There's also a panic button."

Her perusal ended on the only bed in the medium-size single room.

He stepped up beside her, brushing his hand against her upper arm.

She turned and looked at him, noticing the amused smile on his lips, lips she didn't seem to be able to stop staring at.

"I'll take the chair in the corner. It reclines, in case you were wondering."

"Oh." Heat enveloped her body, burning in her core and surging out to her limbs. Confinement made her nervous, and limited her options. Confinement with a man as desirable as Royce turned her nerve endings upside down. "You were saying there's a panic button?"

"Yes, right here in the kitchen."

She followed him into the small space, defined by a three-by-six grid of white tile.

He ran his hand up under the edge of the countertop in

front of the sink, took her hand in his and made her feel the small hidden button.

"It works like a silent alarm in a bank. Press it and the signal goes directly to the police station. Help will arrive within a couple of minutes."

"Good to know." She pulled her hand back, riding a wave of desire. "That must be the bathroom." She crossed the room, pulled open the only other door in the apartment and looked into the full bath.

"It's nice." She closed the door and turned back around, watching Royce open the refrigerator and stare inside. "Would you like something to drink? There's soda and juice."

"No, thanks, I'm fine."

The air in the room hummed with tension. Tension she could feel slide over her skin and drag her toward him.

"On second thought, ice. Is there any ice?"

He opened the freezer compartment. "Yes, do you want some?"

"Please." She stepped into the kitchen and opened the cupboard door above the single sink. It was her best guess for where the glasses might be. Bingo. She took one out and handed it to him, listening to the clink of the cubes as he dropped them in one by one.

He closed the door and held the glass out to her. "Would you like something over them?"

She reached out for it, brushing his cool fingers in the handoff.

Heat smoldered in his eyes as he studied her. The intensity in his gaze sucked the breath right out of her lungs. She let her stare fall to his lips, then back up to his eyes. "Just ice."

They'd been flirting with this for a while. Feeling the pull of a desire that forced them closer to a precipice with every touch, every kiss, every glance. Swift, urgent, undeniable.

She could no longer resist his brand of temptation, didn't want to. She put the glass down on the counter.

Surrender.

"I vowed to keep you safe." Royce advanced on her, praying she'd resist, but she stood her ground, staring up into his face, her lips slightly parted, sexy as hell.

He saw the sheen of sweat form along her collarbone just above the swell of her breasts, under her T-shirt.

"You're safe with me, Adelaide, but we're not safe from this." He reached for her in a rage of need that flared and heated his body.

He pulled her against him, hearing her breathing escalate as he fingered her chin and raised her mouth to his. He took her lips, parting them with his tongue.

Hunger robbed him of coherent thought. He wanted to feel her skin against his, taste the sweet hollows over every inch of her body until he was satisfied, then taste them again.

She moaned, a pleasure rattle deep in her throat. He pulled back for an instant and stared down into her face.

Her eyes shone like dark jade, her cheeks spotted in the heat of desire. He watched her struggle for control over the same need as he did.

"Tell me to stop, Adelaide. Tell me you don't want what I want, and I'll stop. As much as it kills me, I'll never touch you again."

"That would be a crime." She went for the front of his shirt, undoing the first button and fingering the second.

Reaching up, he stilled her hand against his chest. "Are you certain?"

"Yes."

Surrender.

The flood gate opened inside him, and he took her mouth again, broke the kiss and waited for her to finish what she'd started. When the last button popped out of its loop, he reached for her T-shirt and pulled it up over her head, then dropped it on the floor at their feet.

He shed his shirt, watching her reach for the front clasp on her bra.

His breath caught in his throat, in unison with the pop of the opening. He reached for the two halves and pulled them back to expose her breasts. He went to his knees in front of her and took a nipple into his mouth, ringing it with his tongue as she pressed harder against him.

His body responded with crushing need. He went hard and rose to his feet.

She looked up at him, a sexy smile on her mouth as she brushed her hand down his chest one excruciating inch at a time, until she reached the button on his pants, unfastened it and slid the zipper down on his fly.

Royce clamped his teeth together to keep from losing it. Every muscle in his body was cranked down hard. In one swift motion, he picked her up. She spread her legs and wrapped them around his waist. He aimed for the bed, cupping her sweet round bottom in his hands as he reached the edge of the bed.

"Stand up," he whispered as he lifted her up onto the edge.

Adelaide found the bedspread with her toes and rocked back onto her feet, keeping her hands on his broad shoulders as she steadied herself. She let go and watched him slide his pants down over his hips and kick them off.

Her breath came in short, excited gasps, her gaze sliding over the measure of his need. She closed her eyes in anticipation and felt his hands on the opening of her jeans.

Her body hummed, singing for his touch, for the feel of him inside her.

She opened her eyes and smiled down at him.

His eyelids were half-closed, but he stared back, a seductive grin on his lips. Reaching inside her jeans from behind, he smoothed them down over her bottom and pushed them into a tangle at her feet. She pulled one foot out, and with the other she kicked them onto the floor.

"Wanna keep going?" he asked as he hooked his fingers into the waistband of her silk panties.

Heat exploded inside her. "There's no way I'm letting you quit now. You started this, you're going to finish it."

"I'd love to." Royce began the long slide past the point of no return, working her panties down to her exquisite ankles, where she kicked them off and stood naked in front of him.

"Beautiful," he whispered, pulling in one labored breath after another. In even rhythm he smoothed his hands over her body with a measure of control he didn't feel.

He'd explode if he didn't take her soon, but it wasn't his pleasure he craved.

She quivered against him as he grasped either side of her hips and pressed his tongue into her folds, vibrating it across her sex until she cried out and shuddered like a cold kitten.

"Mmm," she whispered as she flopped back on the bed wearing nothing but a smile.

Satisfied for the moment, he shucked off his briefs and lay down beside her, pulling her against him. Feeling her smooth skin, he kissed the side of her neck and ran his hands up her flat belly and over her taut nipples, roughing one with his thumb, then the other until she moaned and reached for his erection, wrapping her hand around him.

He rolled toward her and pulled her underneath him. She opened for him as he raised up and met her gaze.

His control vanished, fried in a blaze of heat that rivaled the sun.

Pushing with one even stroke, he penetrated her.

She gasped. Her arms came up around his back as he buried himself inside her.

Adelaide closed her eyes, letting the age-old art of love-making take her to a new place, a higher place than she'd ever experienced before. A place Royce easily pushed her toward, with slick, sweet precision. His breath was hot against her ear, his words meant only for her to hear.

Her climax built, friction stacked on friction, until she arched against him, gasping, letting pleasure spread through her like wildfire.

A final deep thrust and he came with her, riding the wave of satisfaction as they both found what they were looking for in each other's arms.

Minutes passed. The heat cooled. He gently pulled out of her, rolled onto his side and tucked her in against him.

In the space between them, silence. She liked that. The calm after the storm. She closed her eyes and felt the first measure of real peace she'd experienced in weeks.

Royce laid his cheek against her head on the pillow and pulled the sweet scent of her hair into his lungs. His heart squeezed in his chest, and he tried to name the emotion flaring in his veins.

He'd always known there would be a price to pay if he caved in to his need for her. He just hoped they didn't pay with their lives.

It was happening again.

Adelaide fought the overwhelming sensation and burrowed deeper into her pillow, but the image in her head wouldn't be denied. It came again...and again...stronger...more persistent, until a full picture moved through her consciousness, demanding, pressing...horrifying.

She jolted up in bed, glancing around the small, unfamiliar room, until her gaze settled on Royce, asleep next to her on his side. Her cheeks scorched, and an ache took root deep down in her belly. She reached out and brushed her hand across his shoulder, thinking about the bond that had taken place between them.

Soul mates, Miss Marie had said. They were soul mates.

Pulling in a breath, she threw back the covers and climbed out of bed, in search of her sketch pad. The only light in the one-room studio came from a night-light plugged into an outlet in the kitchen.

"Adelaide? What is it, what's wrong?" Royce sat up.

"I just saw her face, Royce. Victim number three if we can't find her in time."

She spotted the pad lying on the table and hurried to retrieve it, grabbing the pencil next to it before she returned to the bed, turned on the lamp and crawled in under the covers beside him.

Hand shaking, she flipped open the cover of the sketch pad and smoothed it back, staring at the blank page for an instant. Then she began to draw.

Royce sat still, feeling the vibe of tension in her body. A body he'd enjoyed ravishing time and again, with results that blew his mind. She was like a drug in his system, and he wanted more, but he had to go cold turkey.

Looking down at the paper, he watched an image begin to materialize with each stroke of her pencil.

Hair fanned out around the victim's face, a face that now had features. Large, round eyes, open and fixed, a straight nose dotted with freckles. How was it even possible? How did she do it? She was extraordinary, in more ways than one.

Royce closed his eyes, listening to the rub of the pencil on the page. His heart rate accelerated, speeding up with each passing second. On the other side of this night was another victim. Another woman whose life could depend on whether or not he was able to put together the pieces of the puzzle in time. He had to get focused.

Do his job.

"Finished," Adelaide whispered.

He opened his eyes and stared down at the sketch. "What color are her eyes?"

"Blue."

"We'd better get to the station and see if I can convince the chief to put this out to the media. That's the only way we're going to find out who she is before she turns up missing. We need the public's help to identify her."

A knot formed in the pit of his stomach as he pushed back the covers and swung his legs over the edge of the bed, feeling a wave of regret for the necessary turn that needed to take place between them. He was too close.

The pressure of Adelaide's hand on his back pulled him up short, and he paused, turned and reached for her, pulling her onto his lap, cradling her in his arms. He looked down into her face while he languished in the feel of her skin against his one more time.

"You don't have to be sorry for what happened between us tonight. I'm not." She smiled up at him.

"'Sorry' isn't a harsh enough word for what I've done. I betrayed my oath to protect you, and I'll keep betraying it if we don't get out of here."

Her smile faded, her eyes narrowing as she reached up and smoothed her left hand along his jaw. The intimate gesture shook his resolve, dialed it back a notch, and allowed a surge of desire to escape his control for an instant.

Leaning down, he kissed her mouth, jerked back and slid her over onto the bed next to him.

No skin-on-skin contact was the best place to start.

He stood up, determination flooding his brain and offering cover for his single underlying need.

Her.

"Please don't say that. You haven't violated your oath." She reached out, took the covers and pulled them up, covering her naked breasts.

The tightness in his groin eased.

"I'd be dead right now if it weren't for you."

His mouth went dry. "So this was payback for services rendered?"

"No. The two aren't even remotely linked."

"Sex is complicated. Do you want to use the shower first?" he asked.

She shook her head and glanced up at him, her green eyes going wide, a mixture of disbelief and indignation sparking a fire in them. She raised her chin and glared at him.

Regret burned through him, and he felt like such a jerk. Hell, he deserved her anger. He'd intentionally built distance between them by crushing her sense of propriety. He turned for the bathroom and an ice-cold shower.

"Guess I'll go first." He snagged his slacks off the floor and stepped into the bathroom.

Better now than after he had time to analyze the thick emotion she stirred in his blood. Better now than in the heat of a life-and-death situation clouded by passion that could alter the outcome.

It was better now.

ADELAIDE MISMATCHED ROYCE'S strides, taking a couple for every one of his, as they walked down Royal Street headed for the station less than a block away.

Royce was on his cell phone, talking to Detective Hicks. She heard him say goodbye and close his phone.

It was 4:00 a.m. and her nerves were still raw, laid open to seethe, stew and digest his insult, until she made the decision to let it go for now. Call it pleasure for pleasure's sake.

She clutched the sketch pad close to her body as they

passed a couple of unsavory-looking bums on the corner of Royal and Saint Louis streets.

Royce took hold of Adelaide's upper arm, steering her around them, but he didn't let go and the contact reignited her need for his touch, even though she felt like pulling away.

They crossed Conti and entered the station via the front door.

A uniformed officer looked up from behind his position at the front desk. "Hey, Beckett."

"Can you get Chief Danbury on the phone? Tell him we've caught a break in the serial case?"

"Sure."

"Thanks. We'll be upstairs waiting it out in division."

The officer nodded and picked up the telephone receiver.

Royce steered her to the elevator, and didn't let go of her upper arm until the doors opened and they'd stepped inside. She was safe here in the station, but outside, he wasn't so sure. Something about the two men they'd passed loitering on the street corner gave him pause, but he couldn't put his finger on it. Maybe he'd arrested them in the past?

"You're going to tell Danbury about my ability, aren't you?"

His mouth went dry as he stared down into her face. "I can't suppress it. I don't have a choice, Adelaide, when the sketch could save her life."

The look of betrayal in her eyes clutched at his sense of right and wrong but he held his ground. "Results. You provide this department with results. Danbury doesn't care how you obtain them as long as it's legal. He just cares that his officers are making arrests based on the composites you draw."

She shrugged her shoulders and stared up at the lit numbers above the doors. The chimes sounded and the doors slid open. Royce followed her out into the corridor and through the entrance to the detective division.

"I suppose you're right," she said. "It was only a matter of time before Danbury found out."

He was glad she'd reasoned it out, but there was still a tone of betrayal in her acceptance, and responsibility for that, he knew, rested solely on his head for violating the code of conduct, bringing his full-on emotions into the mix and taking her to bed.

"Want some coffee?"

"Yeah. I need to wake up." She plopped into the chair in front of his desk and opened her sketch pad.

Royce fiddled around at the coffee bar, killing time before he had to look into her sleepy eyes again. Just the thought of making love to her had sent his libido off on a tangent he was still working to pull back from.

The sound of footsteps in the hallway brought his head around and he saw Detective Hicks step into the room wearing sweats and a beanie.

"I'm not even on shift for three more hours, Beckett, and you interrupted my morning run. This better be worthwhile."

He picked up the two cups of coffee and headed for his desk. "It is. Come on over and we'll talk standard operating procedure for how we save this woman and catch whoever is responsible."

Hicks snagged a chair from a nearby desk and pulled it over. "I'm listening."

Royce put the cups on his desk and sat down in his chair, watching as Adelaide picked hers up and sat back.

"The coroner determined the killer injected each victim with succinylcholine. What's the scoop on that?"

"It's a paralytic drug, with no antidote. It induces total paralysis, the victim remains conscious, all within thirty seconds. But it causes suffocation within six minutes if the patient doesn't receive RSI, or Rapid Sequence Intubation."

"Yeah, so we need EMS in standby mode with the protocol, or it doesn't matter how fast we get to her, she'll die."

Hicks nodded. "I'll brief the EMS director and we'll inform the ambulance crews of the most likely medical emergency at any potential crime scenes."

Detective Lawton walked into the detective division, followed three minutes later by Chief Danbury, who went directly to the coffee bar.

Nervous tension skated across the back of Royce's neck. He stood up and walked over to Danbury.

"Good morning, Chief."

Danbury held a sugar container over his cup and started to pour. "That depends on what you've got for me, Beckett."

The chief tipped the sugar upright, plunged a stir stick into his cup and met him eye to eye. "So why don't you tell me, and we'll have a sit-down over it, come up with a strategy."

"It's about Adelaide."

Danbury looked over his shoulder at her. "Nice young woman. Does a hell of a job for us."

Royce swallowed, trying to dig the right words out of his vocabulary. Words that wouldn't make her sound like a freak.

"She put together a composite on the next victim."

"Nobody told me they'd found her." Danbury's voice went up an octave. "Where, when?"

"It's a prediscovery sketch, Chief."

"What the hell are you talking about, Beckett?"

Frustrated, he brushed his hand over his head and turned slightly, catching Adelaide's full-blown grimace. "Maybe it would be easier if I showed you...in your office. In private, on a need-to-know basis."

"Damn straight." Danbury picked up his cup of coffee

and headed for his office on the main floor. "You've got ten minutes, Beckett. After that, you've got trouble."

Caution beat a rhythm in him as he walked to his desk, pulled out the bottom drawer and removed the sketches. Proof positive of her extraordinary abilities.

Glancing up, he tried to give Adelaide a reassuring nod, but she didn't look away from her conversation with Detective Lawton. He could live with her anger, as long as she was okay, and alive.

He picked up the sketch pad off the desk and hurried out of the division on Danbury's heels.

"THANK YOU FOR COMING to this impromptu press conference." Chief Danbury stood behind the podium that had been erected on the steps of the police station less than an hour ago, after phone calls went out to the media.

"In recent weeks, two young women have been murdered. We're doing everything possible to catch the person, or persons, responsible, but we need your help to locate the woman we feel could be the next victim." Danbury held up the sketch.

"It's imperative that we find her. A special hotline has been set up to take your calls if you believe you know who this woman is." He rattled off the hotline phone number.

Sweat welled up under Royce's shirt collar and tie and trickled down his back. Standing as backfill behind the chief along with a quarter of the department's officers certainly made them look good, but the consolidation of body heat was torture.

The air temperature was already reaching swelter level, and being the focus of cameras only made it worse.

He pulled in a breath and reached over, putting his hand against the small of Adelaide's back. She didn't pull away, a fact he found encouraging, since her anger didn't seem to have worn off much.

He stared out into the sea of cameras and beyond, spotting a couple of homeless men standing on the other side of Royal Street watching the gathering.

Recognition in need of confirmation spurred him into action. He leaned over and spoke into Adelaide's ear.

"Do you see those two men across the street?"

"Yes."

"Didn't we pass them this morning?"

He watched her focus on them. "Yes. I just remember they both had on nice loafers. Kind of weird if you're homeless."

That was it, that was the small detail he'd noticed on a subconscious level, the one that jacked his heart rate and released anxiety into his bloodstream.

"Did you notice that one of them had a small scar on his lip?"

She looked over and up at him. "Like the one in the drawing I did of the man who took your sister?"

"Yes."

"I only glanced at his face for a second." Her eyes narrowed in contemplation. "But, yeah. He did have a scar on the right-hand corner of his mouth."

"Stay put. You're safe in this crush of uniforms. Scream if you feel threatened for any reason. I'm going after him."

Concern attached to Adelaide's nerves as she watched Royce excuse himself through the group of cops and exit on the right. She watched him pause on the corner of Royal and Conti about the time the two men saw him.

They turned and walked away, headed for Bienville Street, then broke into a jog halfway down the block.

A second later, Royce followed, and she lost sight of him as he took a right onto Bienville.

"And so I want to assure the good citizens of New Orleans

that they're safe, and we will catch whoever is responsible for these heinous murders."

"Chief Danbury, Rachel Wilson, WGNO-TV. An anonymous source has told me there may be a voodoo sect involved. Can you verify this information and tell us what the nature of the serial killings is? In addition I'd like to know if you've been able to establish any significance in the manner in which the bodies are being posed?"

"I'm sorry, Miss Wilson, but we're not going to take any questions at this time. We'll be updating the public as information becomes available." The chief stepped back from the podium.

Adelaide stared down at her watch. Ten minutes. Ten minutes since Royce had turned the corner onto Bienville. She couldn't wait another second. She broke from the cluster of cops and headed straight for Danbury, catching him before he reentered the station door.

"Sir."

"Miss Charboneau. Let me assure you that your job is safe. Royce told me—"

"Listen...please listen. Royce took off after a suspect, and he hasn't come back. I'm worried."

Danbury clutched her elbow. "Where did he go?"

"He headed right on Bienville at the corner." Her heartbeat pounded in her ears, her imagination working overtime with scenarios that made her blood run cold. "We've got to go and find him."

"Go inside. Wait. We'll track him down."

Danbury signaled Detective Hicks, Detective Lawton and a uniformed cop she recognized as Officer Brooks. They huddled around the chief while he briefed them.

Adelaide watched the men break formation and hurry down the steps, across the street and make the corner at Bienville.

Where was Royce? She felt suddenly alone, even surrounded by twenty of the department's finest. She needed Royce, almost as much as she needed air.

In the crowd of cops, one of their radios broke squelch.

"Dispatch, unit one. Do you copy?"

Adelaide strained to hear, stepping closer, as Danbury's familiar voice came in over the transmission.

"Copy unit one, go ahead."

"We need an ambulance at Bienville and Bourbon Streets. We've got an officer down. I repeat, officer down."

Chapter Twelve

The horrifying words coming from the police radio pounded in Adelaide's eardrums.

Her knees went weak. Was it Royce? Dear God, was it him? She had to get to him. Now.

Filtering her way through a sea of blue, she took the steps two at a time and encountered Officer Brooks at the bottom, barring her way.

"Miss Charboneau. Danbury gave me strict instructions that you're to remain safely inside the station."

Frustration jumbled her nerves and gave her gumption she didn't know she had. "Let me pass. If it's Detective Beckett, I need to see him. He may have information from the attack that I can sketch."

The officer cocked his head and studied her.

"Please. Just take me over there, it's only a block away."

"I'm sorry, Miss Charboneau, I have my orders."

"Screw your orders, I'm going!" She dodged past him and broke into a run, hearing his footfalls pound the sidewalk right behind her.

"Adelaide, wait!"

But she didn't wait. She kept moving, across Royal and down Bienville, making the scene at the same time as the ambulance did from the Bourbon Street side.

She pressed through the crowd, ducking and nudging until

she burst into the middle and came face-to-face with Chief Danbury.

"Is it Royce?" Frantic, she leaned sideways and looked around the chief, seeing Royce on the pavement. The front of his white shirt spattered with blood.

Her breath hung up in her throat, and she lunged forward, missing the chief's protective arm as he put it out to stop her.

"Royce!" She went to her knees beside him and watched him open his eyes.

"Adelaide. You shouldn't be here, it's not safe."

Reaching out, she brushed her hand down his arm.

"I'm going to live. With some stitches in my head, I'll be fine." He reached up, snagged her hand and laced his fingers through hers. "Calm down."

A couple of EMTs parted the crowd and she was forced to vacate her place next to him. Standing up, she backed up next to Chief Danbury and watched as they assessed Royce's condition.

"Did anyone see what happened?" Detective Hicks asked. "Stick around if you did. If you didn't, move along, the show is over."

A collective grumble went through the bystanders as they peeled off a couple at a time, until only a handful remained.

Hicks pulled out his notepad and approached a young couple for an eyewitness account.

Adelaide refocused on Royce, watching the EMTs assess a gash on his forehead and one on his scalp. "We'll take you in to get these stitched. Did you lose consciousness?"

"I might have the first time he hit me with that damn pipe."

"You'll need to be observed for a head injury." The female EMT pulled a penlight out of her shirt pocket and shined it in

Royce's eyes. "Equal and reactive. Let's get a C-collar on him and package him for transport to Tulane Medical Center."

In all of the commotion, Adelaide stayed focused on Royce, already picking up the details of the men's faces. The two men he'd chased down Bienville Street. The man with a distinctive scar at the right corner of his mouth. A marking that mirrored the one on the sketch she'd drawn of his sister's abductor.

They loaded Royce onto a gurney and strapped him down.

She turned and stared at Danbury. "I'm going with him."

He nodded. "I'll get Officer Brooks to roll behind you in a squad car. He can haul you both back to the station."

"Thank you." She turned and followed the gurney as the EMTs pushed it to the ambulance and rolled Royce inside. She followed behind and climbed in, itching for her sketch pad and the chance to put together the composite they were going to use to nail these guys.

ROYCE PUNCHED THE ENTRY CODE into the keypad on the back door of the station and escorted Adelaide inside.

"Let's head straight for your office. I don't think I can take any ribbing from the guys for resembling Frankenstein, until I get the face of the bastard who did it out of my aching head and onto paper."

"At least the assault took care of the need to run his composite through an aging program."

"Yeah. I guess there are advantages to having your head split open." He sobered as they reached the elevator and pressed the up button. "It's him, Adelaide. I know it's the man I saw abduct my little sister twenty-nine years ago."

She reached out and brushed his arm, a reassuring gesture that produced an ache in his body. A need for more.

The doors opened and they stepped inside, turned and watched them close.

Alone at last, Royce thought as he turned toward her and grasped her upper arms in his hands. It was a move that churned up heat in his body that wouldn't dissipate.

"I'm sorry I had to explain to Danbury what you do, but he took it well, and because of you, we've got a chance to save lives and stop these nut jobs from killing more innocent women."

"You don't have to apologize, Royce. I know why you did it. It was only a matter of time before my secret came out. It's too bad it took a slime like Clay Franklin to discover it and set this whole thing in motion, instead of leaving me the decision to step up and claim it."

"It was set in motion a long time before Clay figured it out. It went into motion the day you were born and your birth mother left you in that church. That part of the revelation is still yours to reveal." Need pulsed in every cell of his body, but he resisted the urge to pull her against him.

Adelaide pondered his summation, wondering down deep why he didn't wrap his arms around her right now, because that's what she wanted. That's what she needed to chase away the degree of apprehension skating over her nerves.

The elevator hovered to a stop and the doors opened. They stepped out and headed down the hallway to her office.

Halfway there she spotted a flat square box propped against her office door.

"Are you expecting a package?"

"No."

Caution moved her forward at a turtle's pace, while Royce jumped three strides ahead of her and stopped at the door. He knelt next to the parcel and cocked his head to read the label. "No return address, but it's postmarked New Orleans." He stood up. "You're sure you're not expecting anything?"

"Absolutely."

He pulled his cell phone from his belt and moved her back down the hallway toward the elevator. "Chief, Beckett here.

We may have a situation on the third floor. There's a suspicious package in front of Miss Charboneau's office door." He paused. "Okay, I'll look for them in ten." He closed his phone.

"What's going on?" She couldn't keep the tremble out of her voice as she stared up at him, at the hard set of his jaw and the narrowing of his eyes.

"It could be an explosive, Adelaide. The bomb squad is en route to check it out."

He pressed the down button. The carriage arrived and the doors opened. They stepped inside, but this time he opened his arms to her, and she gladly moved into them for the ride down to the main floor.

The elevator doors opened on a mass evacuation from the station.

Danbury spotted them and headed straight for them before they'd even exited the cubicle.

"Hell of a time for this to happen, Beckett. The hotline phones are ringing off the hook, and we'll be standing in the street when the case-breaking call comes in."

"Then they'll call back, Chief. If it's legit, they'll call back."

Danbury grunted and pointed at the front door. "Mandatory evacuation. The bomb squad is bringing in the portable X-ray to scan the package, ETA five minutes."

Royce nodded and steered Adelaide for the main entrance, wondering if the timing of the suspicious package and the opening of the hotline weren't somehow related. The relative link sent a wave of caution surging through him, raising him up on the crest of an unsettling thought.

The timing would require calculation on the part of the killer, which meant he'd have to be totally tuned in to everything transpiring in the case. Could they be dealing with a killer on the inside? Or just someone leaking information to the outside?

They walked out the front of the building into the early-afternoon heat.

Royce scanned the faces of the boys in blue, but he couldn't get his head around the idea that one of them was a killer, or the mastermind behind the search, assault and murder of anyone they suspected of being a Beholder.

Instinctively, he reached for Adelaide and guided her down the steps, where they blended into the crowd and turned to watch the bomb squad enter the building with their high-tech equipment in tow.

HALF AN HOUR LATER, CHIEF Danbury worked his way to the top of the steps, closed his cell phone and gave the all-clear sign. The officers filtered back into the building, but Danbury waited.

Royce made eye contact with him and instantly knew something was up.

"Hey, Chief, tell me the package contained a box of candy and a thank-you note to Adelaide for sketching some creep's face."

"Nada on both counts. They've got the contents laid out in the hallway, and we need Adelaide to tell us if she knows what any of it means."

Tension looped through Adelaide's body and pulled her muscles tight. Only Royce's hand against her back offered a decisive measure of reassurance she could feel.

"What are the items, Chief?" she asked as they followed him through the double doors, which had been propped open.

"Some sort of mask that looks like it came from Mardi Gras, and the damndest thing. A piece of hair bound in a rubber band. I haven't seen the things, but the bomb tech said there's a note attached to the hair."

A chill cultivated under her skin and blossomed on her

arms in the form of gooseflesh. "That's a new wrinkle. Was the hair cut, or pulled out?"

"I don't know." Danbury led the way to the elevator, and they stacked up behind a group of waiting cops. "That'll be a determination for the lab to make. Any idea why someone would send this bizarre stuff to you? It's obviously a message of some kind."

Royce really hadn't told the chief everything. He'd left Danbury believing that this was precipitated by her ability to pull images from victims' thoughts. He'd left her with a measure of privacy, and the decision of whether or not the circumstances warranted revelation of the rest of the story.

Respect latched onto her image of the man standing next to her, protecting her, holding her…caring for her?

"About the message, Chief. There are some additional things you need to know about me."

"Do they require a sit-down?"

"Yes, sir. I believe they do."

They followed the group of officers into the cubicle.

"One thing at a time, or my head might explode. Let's take a look at the package contents, then we'll talk."

"Fair enough." Leaning back against Royce in the tight confines of the elevator helped her to relax, and she pulled strength from his nearness. Wherever the clues ultimately took them, he'd be there beside her, watching over her, keeping her safe.

The doors opened on the second floor and the uniformed cops eased out into the corridor, including Officer Brooks, whom she hadn't noticed until now.

"Miss Charboneau," he said, nodding to her as he exited the elevator.

She owed Brooks an apology for her rude behavior this morning. She'd have to catch up with him later.

The doors slid closed.

"Brooks is a fan of yours, Adelaide. He's up to speed on

this case, and has been my acting intermediary between Hicks in the detective unit and myself. He'll make detective within the year if he stays on track."

"That's nice."

Caution all but roared in Royce's brain. It fit. It fit tight, and sweet, and close. The leak within the department. The source that sent the media running to every scene. Could it be Brooks was bucking for a detective slot?

The elevator stopped on the third floor and they stepped out into the hallway, spotting the open package on the floor, sitting on a white evidence cloth.

"It's a Songe mask, just like the one we found at Clay Franklin's place." He knelt next to it. Adelaide bent closer, staring at the long strands of dark hair clutched in a rubber band, with a slip of paper tucked under it.

Her knees buckled, but Danbury caught her before she went down.

She pulled in a breath and regained her composure, even though her insides were twisting in knots.

"This lock of hair belongs to your mother. You are next." Royce read the words on the paper out loud.

"Do you think it's true?" she asked.

He came to his feet next to her. "I don't know. But if there's a follicle on any one of the hairs, and it's not degraded, Gina might be able to get a myocardial DNA match, using you as an absolute."

"Do either one of you want to tell me what the hell's going on?"

"It's about that sit-down, Chief. The sooner the better."

The elevator doors opened and Officer Brooks charged out like a bull out of the gate. "Chief Danbury. They need you downstairs immediately. A woman is in your office. She claims the woman in our sketch is her next-door neighbor."

Danbury shook his finger in Royce's face. "I'm not done with you, Beckett."

He turned and followed Brooks back to the elevator.

Royce didn't suck in a clear breath until the doors closed. "We'll get Gina on this. Put a rush on it, and maybe we'll get lucky."

Adelaide stepped around the ugly mask and the strands of hair she wanted to finger in the worst way. She opened her office door and stepped inside. "Come on, we've got time to pull the sketch before we head out for our redress."

"A glutton for punishment, aren't you?" He followed her in.

She picked up a sketch pad and pencil from the table and sat down in her chair. "The man with the scar is a significant piece of the puzzle. If we find him, we could find the man behind the Songe mask that Officer Tansy saw."

Looking irritated, Royce took the cell phone off his belt and punched Gina's number. "Hey. I could use you on the third floor outside Adelaide's office. We've got evidence that needs a rush job. Can you handle it? Thanks." He closed his phone, pulled out a chair and sat down, staring across the table at her.

"I'm not tracking with you, Adelaide. I never even saw the guy who hit me. He came out of nowhere, and I was focused on the other two. The one with the scar in particular."

"I got that part, so just describe his face to me, Royce, and I'll help you understand."

Amusement fired in his dark eyes, accentuated by a smirk that crossed his lips and vanished as he leaned forward. Her pencil started to move before he started to speak, a fact that unnerved him, but he kept talking, even closing his eyes to let the scene play out again and again in his mind's eye. He listened to her flip the page in the sketch pad and draw some more, then stop.

"You can look now."

His eyes flicked open, and he stared at her. "You're amazing, Adelaide Charboneau. A keeper."

She grinned and tore two sheets out of the sketch pad, put one down on the table, then pushed it over practically under his nose.

"How did you do this?" He stared at the depiction of what had taken place in the street, noting the details he'd missed. A street vendor at the head of the alley selling masks. A man wearing one, standing next to the cart with a piece of pipe in his hand. The man with the scar at the right-hand corner of his mouth, turning to look back over his shoulder. His partner's retreating back.

"Do you see him?"

"Yeah. He was standing right there. Wearing the same mask as Officer Tansy saw the night he was assaulted."

"Now do a comparison between these two sketches." She slid the drawing of the man who'd abducted his sister across the table.

Royce's breath hung up in his lungs. "They're one and the same."

"So let's find out who he is. There has to be a link to the man wearing the mask, otherwise, why would he risk being caught by trying to kill you with a pipe? They have to be in this together. Catch one, and we catch the others."

"I love the way your mind works." He reached across the table and cupped her cheek for an instant.

"Hmm." Gina's voice from the doorway brought his head around, and he pulled back. Caught like a kid with his hand in the candy jar.

"Is this the urgent evidence that needs examination?" She raised her eyebrows, then lowered them, smiled and turned back out into the hallway.

"I'd be remiss if I didn't tell you it'd be a boon for me if you took that girl off the market, Detective Beckett. She's cramping my style."

Royce was already out of his chair and standing in the

doorway when the comments left Gina's mouth and he hoped like hell Adelaide hadn't heard them.

Gina pulled on a pair of latex gloves and let the band snap against her wrist. Reaching down, she picked up the strands of hair.

"Are there any follicles? Anything you might be able to extract myocardial DNA from?"

"Yeah. I can see a couple. By rush do you mean this afternoon?"

"If possible."

"Who's the absolute?"

"I am." Adelaide stepped past Royce and came face-to-face with Gina. "The hair may belong to my birth mother."

Gina eyed her. "Okay. I need to take a DNA sample." She reached into the pocket of her lab coat and pulled out a wrapped swab. She peeled back the casing, exposing the wooden handle. "Take this and rub it on the inside of your cheek with enough pressure to pick up some cells."

Adelaide pulled the swab out and raked it over the inside of her cheek, took it out and pushed it back into its casing.

"I'll let you know ASAP. What about the mask?"

"Collect it, print it, swab around the mouth. I'm just not sure what its significance is. Fingerprint the box."

"You've got it."

Royce's cell phone rang, and he stepped away to answer it.

"Beckett." The chief's voice came across the line.

"Yeah."

"I want you and Miss Charboneau down here immediately."

"We're on our way." He closed his phone and felt his pulse rate climb. An interesting day was about to turn even more interesting. Especially once he told the chief their case was somehow linked to his little sister's abduction twenty-nine years ago.

Danbury was going to come unglued, and he'd be writing parking tickets over at Jackson Square by week's end.

"We've got to go. Danbury wants us downstairs right now."

Gina cast him a sympathetic glance and returned to evidence collecting.

"Better bring the sketches." He watched Adelaide reenter her office, fold the two drawings, shove them inside the back cover of her pad and grab a pencil.

"Is he still upset?" she asked as they walked toward the elevator.

"We'll find out soon enough." He pointed to the stairwell door, pushed it open, followed her onto the landing and let it snap shut behind him.

"Whatever happens, I'm going to protect you. Badge or no badge, I'll always be there."

She stared up into his face and smiled. "You think Danbury is going to yank your badge?"

"I've withheld information."

"But none of it impeded the investigation."

"That remains to be seen. We don't have all the facts."

Somewhere in the building, a stairwell door popped shut and the sound of footsteps echoed against the concrete.

"Come on, let's go." He took a step away, but she reached out and grabbed his arm.

He stopped and turned toward her, feeling heat rise inside him, burning through his resolve with every passing second.

She rocked up onto her tiptoes and brushed her lips against his. He pulled her against him, feeling the insatiable drive of desire ricochet through his senses.

"For luck," she whispered as she pulled back.

He took her hand and led them down the stairs and out into the bustle on the main floor.

Danbury spotted them and waved through the glass of his

office. There was no escape, and Royce found his nerves were shot by the time he and Adelaide entered the door.

"Mrs. Colby, this is Detective Beckett, and our sketch artist, Adelaide Charboneau."

The middle-aged woman reached out and shook both of their hands. "Nice to meet you. Please, call me Jane."

"Jane is the next-door neighbor of Beth Wendell, the woman we believe is in the sketch."

"We live in the same duplex." She looked away, then back up at them. "She's a very nice woman. Lives alone. Doesn't go out much. That's why it was so strange when a man in a dark-colored car pulled into the driveway, and she left with him."

"I took the liberty of pulling Beth Wendell's driver's licence information and confirmed it."

Royce relaxed slightly and grabbed a couple of chairs for Adelaide and himself. "Jane, is there any chance you can remember what the car looked like?"

"It was so dark. We don't have a streetlight. I don't know what kind of car it was. I'm sorry."

"Thank you. Call if you remember any detail, no matter how small. It will help us." Royce sat back in his chair.

"Jane got a good look at the man Beth Wendell left with last night. I was hoping she could describe him to you, Miss Charboneau, and we could get a composite."

"Certainly." Adelaide got comfortable in the chair and opened her pad. "Go ahead and describe him to me in as much detail as you can remember."

Jane Colby closed her eyes and started to talk. Adelaide put her pencil to the paper and started to draw.

Her heart rate pumped up. Breathe…just breathe, she reminded herself as she completed the sketch and began to scribble in the background so Jane Colby wouldn't freak out because she was already finished. She knew the face in the drawing. Knew the telltale scar at the right corner of the man's mouth.

"That's all I remember." Jane paused.

"Is this the man you saw?" Adelaide flipped the sketch pad around and watched Jane's eyes widen.

"That's him. It's incredible, it looks exactly like him. How did you do that?"

"I'm a good listener." She tore the sketch out of the pad and handed it to Royce.

"I'll put this out on an APB right now, Chief."

Adelaide clasped her sketch pad to her chest and stood up, thankful she'd just been able to provide Royce with one more piece of evidence.

The one that proved conclusively the cases were linked.

Chapter Thirteen

"His name's Vincent Getty. He has an extensive criminal history, including robbery, assault, eluding officers…and kidnapping. He's one bad guy."

Royce stared out at the uniformed cops in the briefing room, his gaze eventually settling on Adelaide, who sat in the back of the room next to Chief Danbury.

"If you come in contact with him, use extreme caution—odds are he's armed and dangerous. We want to catch him, but we also want Beth Wendell, safe and alive. He could be our only lead to accomplish that."

He reached down and turned off the oversize projection of Vincent Getty's face displayed on the screen behind him. "You all have his mug shot on the briefing flyer, so keep your eyes open out there. You're dismissed."

Royce scooped up his files and made his way to the back of the room. "Are we ready to search Beth Wendell's house?"

"Detective Hicks is on his way with a limited warrant." Danbury cleared his throat. "It's a visible-evidence-only warrant. We need to have all our ducks in a row on this one in case it ends badly."

"We'll meet you in the parking lot." Royce followed the chief and Adelaide out of the briefing room, where he and

Adelaide broke company with Danbury and headed for the detective division.

"Have you called your parents to let them know about Vincent Getty?"

He glanced over at her as he pressed the elevator button. "No. It'll tear my mother up, and make my father angry again. His health isn't so great. He did a lot of grieving for what could have been."

The doors opened and they stepped inside.

"What about your sister, Kimberly?"

"That's tricky. She's fragile. She was always a special needs kid. That's why she wasn't adopted until my parents came along when she was four. The abduction made her problems worse. Digging into it again, putting her face-to-face with the man who terrorized her, could cause her to snap."

He stared at the doors. "I'll cross that bridge when we catch the creep."

The doors opened and they walked down the corridor and into the detective division. The place hummed with an excitement he could feel in his bones. His stare locked on Officer Brooks chatting with Detective Lawton. Why didn't that surprise him? He was gunning for a promotion in the worst possible way. Climbing over the top of a good detective's head.

Royce put the files down on his desk and looked up at Adelaide, watching a slow, sweet smile spread across her perfect lips. His insides went to mush. He wanted to kiss her, to tell her that he'd only pushed her away by insulting her after making love to her for her own protection...and his.

Hicks hurried into the division and came to a stop in the center of the room.

"We've got our limited warrant. Pair up and head to the Wendell residence. The landlord will meet us there to provide access. The address is 4818 Walter Avenue. See you there."

ADELAIDE STOOD IN THE ENTRYWAY of Beth Wendell's duplex, staring at the aftermath of the struggle that had gone on between her and the man with the scar.

A shiver quaked over her body and put her back in the terrifying moments before she'd been dragged from her closet, blindfolded and fighting for her life.

She stared at Royce, and her heart rate slowed. If it weren't for him…

"Beckett, what do you make of this?" Hicks held up an ID badge dangling from a hot-pink lanyard.

"Says she's a student at Tulane. So was victim number one. Could be our guy is picking them up on campus. What about Wendy Davis?"

"Graduated last year from Loyola."

"Damn." Frustration beat a heated path through his body. "There's nothing here. The guy was careful, other than tipping over a few things in the struggle. We'd be better off staking out the dump site on the east. Maybe we'll get lucky and catch them there."

Hicks nodded. "Listen up, people. We're leaving this scene to Gina for a print dust, and we're headed for the GPS dump site out in Algiers. We'll use the car-to-car scrambled frequency on channel forty-two, in case our unsub has a police scanner on board and is listening to our ten-twenty location codes."

Royce followed Adelaide through the doorway and out into the late-afternoon heat. The day was coming to an end, and they weren't any closer to finding Beth Wendell, or the thug with the scar, even though his face was everywhere, including on WGNO-TV's six o'clock news report as a person of interest.

They passed Gina coming up the walk with her fingerprint kit in hand. "Hey." She pulled up short. "Adelaide, I've got some news on the myocardial sample from this morning."

Adelaide's heart nearly pounded out of her chest as she

turned around to face Gina, who sported dark circles under her eyes and a thin smile. "You look overworked, Gina, so thank you in advance."

"Yeah, well, it's a rush-rush world, but whoever wrote that creepy note on the ponytail got it right. Your DNA is a match to the myocardial DNA in the follicles. It belonged to your mother. In case you haven't noticed, you're both wearing the same shade on your head." She turned around and disappeared through the doorway into the house.

Adelaide buried her face in her hands as tears squeezed from her eyes, and her throat constricted so tightly she could hardly breathe.

Royce gathered her in his arms, stroking the back of her head in comfort.

"It's hers, Royce. I can't believe it, after all these years. But where did it come from?" Fear dammed up her emotions, and she uncovered her face, then looked up into his eyes.

"If she's out there, we'll find her, Adelaide. That's the one thing about the past, it's finite, you can't change it, but it leaves you a lot of clues if you're willing to follow them. Come on, let's head for Algiers and grab a burger on the way. I'm starving."

BLADES OF SHADOW KNIFED through the trees on the perimeter of the small park in Algiers. Somewhere in the neighborhood a dog barked incessantly, spooked by some unknown factor in the dark.

Royce glanced down at the glowing hands on his watch—a quarter past midnight. Then over at Adelaide, who sat facing him in his car, her arm resting on the back of the seat and her head on her arm.

She hadn't spoken in at least half an hour, and he reached for her, sliding his hand up her forearm.

"Tired?"

"Uh-huh, but I'll take the chair tonight when we get back to the safe house."

A jolt of desire zapped through him, raising his awareness level to the roof. "No way, I'm all over it."

She snickered, raised her head up suddenly and pointed toward the park. "Look."

Royce refocused on his patch of observation, seeing movement in the brush along the north end of the perimeter. He leaned down and picked up the radio mic. "All units, I've got someone entering the north side of the park."

"Copy that, Beckett."

He watched the single dark patch split and become two people, their movements erratic in the sporadic patches of light. He couldn't be sure, but they seemed to be arguing. He reached up and switched the dome light from auto to off.

"All units, this is Hicks. Move in slowly."

Royce picked up the trail of their movement, his heartbeat escalating with each passing second as adrenaline surged in his veins. "This is it, Adelaide, it stops here...tonight."

"I hope so," she whispered in the darkness.

He watched one of the two people fold to the ground and the other one go to a kneeling position. "All units, one of them is down on the ground. Move in."

"Come on. Stay close." He unholstered his weapon, pulled back the slide and opened the car door, waving her out on his side. He let the door close silently, but not latch.

They crossed the street and entered the park.

Tension roared in his head and tempered his muscles like iron. He reached back and took Adelaide's hand in his free one, feeling a wave of caution wash over him. There were more than one of these creeps. And he still had a job to do where she was concerned. He couldn't let his guard down, not even for a second.

"Move in!" Hicks's attack command sliced through the thick night air.

They rushed forward. Royce let go of Adelaide's hand, brought his up under the butt of his pistol and took aim.

Ten flashlight beams all came on at once as men, guns and light encircled the two people on the ground in the middle of the park.

"Police."

The couple untangled from their lip-lock, fooled with the buttons on their clothes and slowly sat up.

"We didn't do anything, Officer," the kid said in a hoarse voice just above a whisper. "We were just kissing."

"Stand down, everyone," Hicks ordered.

"Did my daddy send you?" The young woman's cheeks burned red-hot in the officers' flashlight beams.

"No, miss, he didn't," Royce said, trying to sound official. "This park's off-limits. It's after curfew, so if you're not home in ten minutes, we'll be forced to arrest you both."

They jumped to their feet and took off in the direction they'd come.

"Dammit," Hicks said, trying not to chuckle. "I thought we had them for sure."

Royce holstered his Glock and glanced around, seeing Detective Lawton running across the park toward them, waving a handheld radio.

"Hicks," he yelled. "You've got to hear this 911 call, it sounds like our missing woman out off River Road."

Royce's hearing went on hyperalert as they gathered around to listen to the radio call. "That's the GPS location on the west."

Hicks looked up at him. "You're right. It's a bait and switch. We've been duped."

"Caller, please repeat your location for me."

"I'm just off River Road. Something's going on out here on the Mississippi side. I'm raccoon hunting, and I saw a couple of guys dragging a woman toward the river. I think she might be dead because she wasn't moving. I'm hunkered down in the brush so they don't see me."

"Stay on the line with me, sir. I'll dispatch the police and an ambulance."

"Okay, but you better hurry."

"I'll remind EMS about the Rapid Sequence Intubation protocol for succinylcholine," Royce said, turning for his car, with Adelaide right next to him.

Detectives scattered like storm clouds and evaporated into the darkness.

Royce and Adelaide broke into a dead run across the park, and made the car. Royce pulled open the driver's-side door and watched Adelaide slide across the seat first.

His heart hammered in his eardrums as he climbed in and fired the engine, praying they got there in time to save Beth Wendell, but another worry ground across his nerves at the same time, putting him on the defensive. The killers were one victim away from Adelaide. *His Adelaide.* And he was no closer to finding them now than he'd been the first night he rescued her. He swallowed hard, hit the gas pedal and roared away from the curb.

RIVER ROAD WAS TEEMING WITH officers and a single emergency vehicle by the time Royce and Adelaide made the twenty-five-minute drive from Algiers, with the grill lights flashing and siren blaring.

They rolled up on the scene and climbed out of the car, spotting Chief Danbury standing next to the ambulance.

"Chief, what's the word?"

"We missed the unsubs by ten minutes. I've got patrol units combing the area. Beth Wendell is alive at the moment. EMS intubated her according to the RSI protocols, but they're not sure if it was soon enough. They're rolling her to Tulane Medical Center. I want Adelaide at the hospital right behind the ambulance, with her sketch pad getting an image from that poor woman. God help us if she dies without waking up."

Adelaide nodded, feeling her mouth go dry. So many lives depended on identifying the suspects. Hers included.

"We're on it." Royce took her elbow and guided her back to the car. They hopped in and flipped a U-turn, falling in behind the emergency vehicle.

"Someone's leaking our information, Adelaide. It's got to be the only way these guys know where we are every step." Royce shook his head in disgust. "They've got someone in the department."

"A dirty cop?"

"Could be. It would explain a lot. Like how the media had the detail about the bodies being posed, and possible voodoo involvement in the ritualistic elements at the scenes. That information wasn't released to the press, or put out on the police radio in case they happened to be listening."

He made the sweeping turn on River Road that moved in close to the Mississippi on the left. "And our stake-out tonight in Algiers, catching a couple of lovesick teens making out in the grass, instead of the killers dumping Beth Wendell. That was no coincidence."

He braked behind the ambulance and followed it in a left-hand turn onto 90. "They simply changed it up and went with the west location knowing we'd be sitting half an hour away waiting for them to show."

He slammed his hand against the steering wheel.

Adelaide started and reached out to stroke his upper arm with her hand, feeling the tension in his biceps. "It makes sense. It explains why we can't get in front of this."

Reaching out, Royce put his hand over hers where it lay on his right arm. The worst of his thoughts he kept to himself, but she had to be thinking it, too.

If the killers stayed true to their established pattern, they were only one victim away from their ultimate goal.

To kill a Beholder.

ADELAIDE STOOD NEXT TO BETH Wendell's hospital bed in the ICU, listening to the respirator work, pumping oxygen into her lungs.

Beth was most likely going to survive. But it had been touch and go from the moment the ambulance had arrived three hours ago until now.

Royce stood at the foot of the bed, looking more agitated than she'd ever seen him before.

"Miss Wendell had a rough go of it. She's lucky to be alive," a nurse said, as she adjusted the IV pump and stepped back. "Ten minutes max."

"Thank you." Adelaide flipped open her sketch pad and gripped her pencil as she listened to the sound of the nurse's rubber shoes on the tile floor. She didn't look up until she heard the door close. Having to explain her abilities tonight was the last thing she needed right now. She just wanted to do her job and go home.

"Beth, I know you can hear my voice. I need your help to catch the people who did this to you." She glanced at Royce, drawing strength from his tired smile and his nod of encouragement.

"I want you to imagine their faces for me. See them in your mind's eye." Her pencil started to move. "Good, Beth."

The images flooded Adelaide's head faster than she could draw them, but there was nothing new in the images that materialized at the point of her pencil. The Songe with the high crest, the man with the scar at the right corner of his mouth. Another man, possibly the one Royce had chased after during the press conference.

"That's very good, Beth. You've done a great job. Rest

now." She shook her head, handed the sketch pad to Royce and slipped the pencil in above her ear.

Tears stung her eyes as he took her hand and led her out of the room, through the door and into the corridor, where he pulled her into his arms.

She had nothing left to give. If defeat was a prescription, she'd taken an overdose. She let the tears come. She let them purge the helplessness inside her, while she felt the strength of Royce's arms holding her back from total collapse.

"Better?" he asked as he pulled back, produced a handkerchief from his pocket and handed it to her.

"Yes. It just seems so hopeless when all I can get are the same images time and time again. It's almost like it's being done intentionally, so the victims and I can't see who's behind the mask. They can't be exposed if I can't see them."

"He's a true believer, Adelaide. He has taken the legend of the Beholders seriously, and is trying to destroy all of them."

A shiver skittered over her body, and she rubbed her hands across her arms. "Can we go? I'm exhausted. If I don't get some rest I'm going to fall over."

"Yeah. That chair is gonna feel like a million bucks tonight."

She nudged him with her elbow as they headed for the elevators.

"I want you to know, Adelaide, I'm a true believer."

The air between them was charged.

"At the beginning of this thing, I couldn't get my head around it. My brain just wouldn't go there. But now—"

"Stop! It's happening again." She grabbed the sketch pad from Royce's hand and pulled the pencil from above her ear. Crumpling to her knees, she put the pad on the floor and started to draw, watching victim number four's familiar face materialize on the page at Royce's feet.

"Oh dear God, it's Gina."

Royce pulled his cell phone out of his shirt pocket and dialed Chief Danbury.

"Chief Danbury here. Tell me Adelaide got us something to go on from Beth Wendell."

"Is Gina on scene?" Royce's muscles cranked tight between his shoulder blades, and a sick sensation moved around in his gut.

"We called her in over three hours ago, but she never showed up. I had to bring in a lead CSI from another parish to process this scene."

"That's because she's victim number four, Chief. Adelaide just sketched her picture."

The line went silent for an instant. "I'll get a team over to Gina's place right now to check it out."

"Hicks should take a team to the park out in Algiers. These nut jobs will follow through with the ritual before they try to get to Adelaide. They'll try to dump her at the GPS coordinates if they can."

"Take her back to the safe house, and lock it down tight. I'll put an extra unit on you both."

"Will do."

The chief hung up.

Royce reached down and helped Adelaide to her feet. "I never saw this coming."

"Gina is a nonconforming victim. Her hair isn't dark, and it's short. Don't you see, you've already disrupted their pattern somehow, and they're scrambling to put it back on track."

He hit the down button on the elevator. "I think it's because she has the snippet of your mother's hair, and somebody wants it back. She's a victim of opportunity that negated their task of finding and kidnapping another woman. They're killing the proverbial two birds with one stone."

Adelaide's blood chilled in her veins as she followed Royce into the elevator. Had giving the lock of hair to Gina forced the killer's reaction?

"What if it's part of the ritual? The destruction of the Beholder?"

"Makes sense. The FBI said the final victim up in Baton Rouge was missing a patch of hair."

Guilt attached to her nerves, and she prayed Royce was wrong. She just couldn't stand the thought of having someone's death on her hands, simply because they'd handled an item the killers believed held some sort of voodoo magic.

Chapter Fourteen

Royce was beat; so was Adelaide, judging by her slow, methodical progression up the stairs leading to the safe house.

He was almost too tired to notice the tantalizing sway of her hips inside her jeans and the shape of her sweet bottom two feet from his face.

Almost.

He stared up at her as he took the last two steps onto the landing where he stopped.

She turned to face him. A seductive smile spread on her lips as their gazes met. He was hooked. He wanted her. Here, now. Tomorrow. Forever.

"Adelaide," he whispered, reaching for her.

She moved into his arms and raised her face to his.

He kissed her, savoring the feel of her mouth. Easing her lips apart with his tongue, he tasted her, until the fire in his blood blazed white-hot and annihilated his control.

Picking her up with his hands locked on her butt, he pressed her against him. She responded by wrapping her legs around his hips, a move that sent his libido into overdrive.

His breathing escalated exponentially, coming hot and heavy in his eardrums. He pinned her against the railing and burned kisses across the bare skin just above her breasts, pulling her sweet scent into his lungs like a starving man.

"What'll the neighbors think?" she whispered against

his hair, stroking her fingers through it with ever-increasing pressure.

"To hell with the neighbors." He pulled back, dug into his pocket and produced the safe house key.

Angling sideways, he unlocked the door, turned the knob and kicked it open with his foot. Stepping over the threshold into the dark room, he reached out and slammed the door shut.

Turning, he aimed for where he knew the bed was and stepped forward.

Whack!

Stunned confusion rocked his brain. Bone-jarring pain vibrated his body and exploded at the back of his skull.

He was falling.

Falling forward, still clutching Adelaide to the front of his chest. At the last second, he cupped the back of her head.

They hit the ground.

A scream ripped from her throat on a whoosh of air right next to his ear as he body slammed her in the dark.

Behind him he heard the faint click of the light switch.

In one horrific second things crystalized in his brain.

They'd walked straight into an ambush.

Vincent Getty stood behind the closed door holding a baseball bat. "What took you two so long?"

The bathroom door flew open and Royce recognized Vincent's cohort from the foot chase, but there was more. He'd seen the thug somewhere else.

"Get his gun."

He brushed back Royce's jacket and snagged his Glock from its holster, then slammed his foot into Royce's ribs.

Royce flinched and gritted his teeth. He'd shield Adelaide for as long as he could.

"Get off. I want to see her."

Royce glanced down at Adelaide. Her eyes were wide

with surprise, and he listened to her try to suck in a normal breath.

Gently he put his hands down on either side of her head and pushed back up onto his knees.

"She doesn't look so scary." The man who'd taken his gun waved it around and slowly brought the barrel down, pointing it straight at her.

Caution roared through Royce as he prepared to throw himself over her and take the nut job's bullet.

It was at the hospital where he'd seen the other guy, dressed in a maintenance uniform and coming out of Officer Tansy's room just before he coded.

"Let's kill her now."

"Not in the plan, buddy. Not in the plan." Vincent stepped closer.

The hair on the back of Royce's neck bristled as he watched Getty's movements, looking for a chance to turn the twisted events his way. Getty wanted Adelaide, just like he'd wanted his sister twenty-nine years ago. He couldn't help his sister as a kid, but he wasn't a kid anymore, and he wasn't going to let them have Adelaide, not without a fight.

A tinny ring of footsteps on the metal stairs outside pulled Vincent's attention away for an instant.

Royce popped to his feet and dove for the man holding his gun, pushing him back into the kitchen. He heard the pistol clatter to the floor in the scuffle and skid across the tile, but he couldn't see it.

Once, twice, three times he slammed his fist into the thug's face. Footsteps behind him warned that the gig was almost up. He pulled the man into a choke hold and whipped around, using him as a shield, and found himself staring down the barrel of a gun.

Lifting his gaze past the deadly weapon aimed at his forehead, he stared into the dark eyes of Officer Brooks.

He might never get another chance. He put his hand back,

fingering the panic button under the lip of the counter, and pressed it.

"You treasonous bastard," he ground out, and inched forward.

A smug smile broke out on Brooks's lips. "Let him go, and get on the ground, Beckett, before I put a bullet in your fat head and take your job."

Royce slowly released the man, who stepped away and went to his knees, then hit the tile hard as Vincent charged over and stomped his foot in the middle of his back, forcing him onto his belly.

"Did you bring it?" Vincent asked.

"Yeah. It's right here."

He heard Brooks's gun slide into his holster.

"But I don't know what you want with a filthy old piece of hair. Now they've got me on surveillance tape entering the lab. How am I going to explain that to Chief Danbury?"

Royce watched the nut job who'd waved his gun around like a toy pick it up again from a spot under the table.

"You're such a complainer, Brooks. And you made your own problem, seeing how you're the one who took it in the first place, along with the mask, and sent them to her so she could find out about her momma." The thug stepped into the kitchen.

"Now wait a minute." Brooks's voice changed in pitch, a sign Royce knew betrayed the increasing level of tension in the situation.

"What about that, Brooks?" Vincent said, reaching for the gun his crazy buddy was holding. Royce's gun.

"Hold on. I've been with you all the way. You wouldn't have half the information about her if I hadn't told you. Who got close enough to turn her cell phone into a tracking device? Me. You need me."

Caution wiggled up Royce's spine. He was in a hell of a bad spot. Bad guys were one thing, but bickering bad guys were worse. He glanced over at Adelaide, who was still on the floor. They made eye contact.

"You've served your purpose, that's why we're done with you."

Pop! Pop!

Royce flinched and turned his head as Brooks dropped next to him. Blood seeped out from under Brooks's body and oozed across the floor toward him.

"What about him? Can I shoot him?"

"No. I've got my orders. A Protector has to die watching us take the Beholder right out from under his hand."

"I like that."

"Search her, would ya? Make sure she doesn't have the gris-gris on her. I don't want to touch the damn thing…and get her cell phone. We don't need it to track her anymore."

Adelaide came up off the floor with one focus, to take Royce's gun and blast some holes in Vincent Getty. But he was ready for her, and he smacked her square in the face with an open palm.

She saw stars, tasted blood in her mouth.

The impact sent her stumbling backward and she caught the edge of the bed with the back of her legs and fell.

Sitting up, she watched in horror as Getty pulled a loaded syringe out of his jacket pocket, flipped the cap off with his thumb and jabbed it into the back of Royce's leg.

Royce came around swinging, but slumped to the floor a second later, eyes wide open and locked on the ceiling overhead.

"Get the Beholder, and let's get out of here," Vincent said, his voice laced with menace.

His cohort grabbed her upper arm and dragged her to her feet.

"Where's the gris-gris?" He shook her until her teeth rattled in her head.

"In my pocket."

He rummaged in her pants pocket, jerked out the doll, tore its head off and flung both pieces of it toward Vincent, who ducked away.

"Dammit, you know I can't touch that thing." Getty kicked it with the toe of his boot and the doll skittered into the corner.

He laughed out loud, fingering the cell phone in her other pocket before he pulled it out, dropping it on the floor and crushing in once with his foot.

Vincent produced a roll of duct tape and tore off a piece. Walking over to where they stood, he slapped it over her mouth. "Scream through that if you wanna."

Tearing off a long piece, he bound her hands behind her back. Grunting as he turned for the door and pulled it open.

Sticking his head out, he took a look. "It's clear. Let's go."

Adelaide fought back, kicking and thrashing, even managing to catch Royce's gun with her toe in the process. It skittered across the floor toward him and hit his shoe, but he didn't move.

Anguish welled inside her, stopping up the air in her lungs.

They dragged her to the door, and she caught one last look at Royce, paralyzed on the floor of the safe house. His system was full of succinylcholine, and he was only minutes from death.

Nausea swelled inside her as the last horrifying image of him imprinted on her brain along with a reality she'd suspected for some time. She was in love with her Protector.

She fought the dread that consumed her as the brute dragged her down the stairs, out into the alley, then around the corner to an old clunker of a car idling at the curb with its driver behind the wheel.

He released the trunk latch.

Adelaide watched the lid come up in slow motion. It was the stuff of nightmares, her nightmares, her depiction of her own murder, and final resting place in the trunk of a car with her throat slit.

Horrified, she dared to look inside her tomb, and found herself face-to-face with CSI Gina Gantz.

Vincent picked her up, stuffed her in the trunk and shut the lid.

ROYCE COUNTED THE SECONDS IN his head to keep from losing his mind as he stared up at the ceiling, unable to move.

The insidious drug was creeping into the muscles of his diaphragm, making it hard to suck in air.

Adelaide. He tried to swallow the saliva that built up in his mouth, triggered by the emotion looping in his head, but he couldn't even do that.

What would happen to her if he didn't make it? Would Hicks and Danbury figure it out in time to save her life? Hell, he hadn't even been able to figure out who the mastermind behind it was, and he still didn't know.

Panic surged inside him as he tried to pull a deep breath in through his nose, but each inhalation was becoming more labored than the one before.

His lungs burned for oxygen.

So this was it. This was death? Slow suffocation. Four minutes to go.

This was hell.

He hadn't told her how he felt about her. He hadn't voiced the sappy words that would be locked on his tongue forever. But worst of all, he couldn't protect her anymore.

The sound of footsteps, hammering against metal steps in droves, filtered through his waning recollection.

Three minutes to go. The light started to dim. He noticed it in the darkness that ringed his peripheral vision and slowly closed in.

Adelaide.

"It's succinylcholine. RSI Intubation protocol. Tube him, bag him, full open O_2 line, at sixteen liters. Start an IV, with five milligrams of Midazolam, and contact medical control for permission to administer point-five milligrams of Atropine if he codes en route—"

The final pinpoint of light he was focused on faded to black. He heard Chief Danbury in the background.

"Call his family, get them to the hospital ASAP."

ADELAIDE GOT HER BEARINGS IN the trunk of the moving car and attempted to roll onto her right side in the cramped compartment.

A muffled cry resulted and she realized she'd pinned Gina against the spare tire.

She sucked in a breath and gagged on the stench of stale gasoline and rubber tires.

Feeling behind her with her limited range of motion, she elicited another cry from Gina as she poked her in the face with her fingers. This was like playing a sick game of Twister.

Careful to not hurt her again, Adelaide picked at the tape covering Gina's mouth and peeled it back.

"Ouch," she whispered.

Adelaide mumbled an apology behind the tape on her mouth.

"I think I can flip around and work on your hands."

"Uh-huh."

"How in the hell did they pull this off?" Gina said, an element of hysteria entering her voice as she struggled to maneuver in the tiny space. "We've got to get out of here."

"Shh," Adelaide hissed in the dark, fearing the attention Gina could bring down on their heads if Getty heard them.

They had fifteen minutes at the most if the GPS location in Algiers was their destination.

Gina kicked her in the head as she leaned forward and wiggled like a worm, squirming around and ending up pressed against her back. "Hang on, I'll roll over and I should be able to find your hands."

Adelaide listened to the pitch of the engine change as the car slowed down. "Mmm."

"Dammit," Gina ground out as she rocked forward with the braking of the car.

Adelaide held her breath, praying it was only a stoplight that stood in the way of freedom, and that the car would accelerate again.

"Adelaide. This could be it. I wasn't born yesterday and I know these guys aren't going to stop. They're going to kill me, but there's something you have to know."

Tears burned the backs of her eyes.

"I've seen the way Royce looks at you. The guy's got it bad, he's head over heels in love with—"

Two car doors opened and closed in unison.

Adelaide squeezed her eyes shut, almost relieved that she couldn't tell Gina that Royce was dead.

The trunk popped open, and she squinted up at the light, making out the dark shape of Vincent Getty silhouetted against a dawn sky.

"You know where and how to pose her. Do you have the GPS unit?"

"Yeah."

"Call us when it's done, and get back to the grotto before dark. The ceremony starts at dusk."

"Okay."

Getty reached into the trunk and pulled her up by the hair.

Behind the tape she screamed as he locked his arms around her torso and wrenched her from the trunk, then slammed it shut.

Chapter Fifteen

Royce opened his eyes, blinked them closed, opened them again and tried to focus, making out shapes and shadows moving around him.

Someone was inside his head with a sledgehammer pounding out a beat that made him want to puke.

"He's waking up."

The sound of his mom Rachel's excited voice snapped him out of the haze he floated in. Maybe he wasn't dead. He closed his eyes, letting his gut settle. He pulled in one even breath after another, putting succinct thought in front of succinct thought.

"Adelaide," he said, tasting her on his tongue.

"Did he say Adelaide?" His mother's question dragged him into full awareness, and he opened his eyes, watching everything come into focus.

"Son?" His dad stood up from a chair to the right of his hospital bed, where he sat next to Royce's sister, Kimberly. "Thank God you're awake. We've been worried about you."

"How long? How long have I been out?"

"Since four in the morning when they brought you in."

He raised his arm and stared at the spot where his watch should have been. "Time?"

His dad glanced down at his watch. "It's almost eight in the morning."

"I've got to get out of here. She could still be alive."

"Royce, what's going on?" his father said. "Push the call button, Rachel, get a doctor in here to make sure he's all right."

Royce stared at the IV line emptying clear liquid into his arm. Reaching for it, he yanked off the tape and almost had the line extracted when a nurse walked into the room with Chief Danbury on her heels.

"What are you doing, Royce?" Danbury asked, staring at him from the foot of the bed as he tapped a case file against his palm.

"Getting out of here. They've got her, Chief. Vincent Getty and his sidekick killed Brooks with my gun, left me for dead at the safe house and took Adelaide."

Reaching out, Royce found the controls and held down the up button. The bed canted him into an upright position, and he attempted to hold still while the nurse took out the IV line.

"Tell me something I don't already know, Beckett."

"Brooks was dirty. He's been leaking information about the case to someone, including the press. They've been two steps in front of us the whole time."

"Any idea who?"

"No. I've got no clue who the mastermind is. Vincent Getty is just the muscle."

The chief's cell phone rang and he answered it, giving the irritated nurse an apologetic shake of his head before turning his back to them and moving out into the corridor.

Royce rubbed the spot where the tape had been and climbed out of bed, liking the feel of the cool floor under his bare feet.

"Where are you going, sir?" the nurse asked as she coiled up the IV tubing and looped it over the IV pump.

"I can't solve this case from bed. She's out there and I have to find her." He attempted to stand, made it up onto his feet, where his dad caught him before he passed out.

His mother gasped. "I'm going to go and get a cup of coffee. Do you want one, Ted?"

"Damn." Royce sat back down on the edge of the bed in frustration, sucking in one labored breath after another until he felt his equilibrium return.

"Take is slow, sir. You almost died four hours ago." The nurse turned and left the room, almost colliding with Danbury in the doorway.

"I'll go with you, Rachel." His father rounded the end of the bed and took his mom's hand.

He glanced over at his sister and caught her grinning.

"That was Hicks checking in with an update. They made it to the park out in Algiers a few minutes behind the thugs who kidnapped Gina. They got to her in time. She's in recovery right now, in better shape than you are, and she says they put Adelaide in the trunk with her, probably at the safe house, but they pulled over before they reached Algiers and transferred her to another vehicle."

Royce's gut fisted, his body responding to the news his heart couldn't quite take. "Anything else, Chief? Does she remember anything that could help us?"

"She did get a quick look before the trunk lid closed. She said she saw a dark blue or black sedan, possibly a Mercedes."

"Sounds like the car Jane Colby described the night Beth Wendell was taken."

"Gina said the motor made a lot of racket, clattering like a truck on the freeway, said she could smell burning diesel fuel. But she overheard Getty say something more ominous."

Royce held his breath, waiting for information he knew wouldn't be good.

"He told the other driver to be back at the grotto before dark for the ceremony."

Caution frayed his nerves. His gaze locked on his sister, Kimberly, a grown woman with the mind of a child. "Have you got the sketch of Getty and the Songe mask that Adelaide drew?"

"Sure do. Right here." Danbury laid the file on the end of the bed, opened it and pulled out the two sketches.

A combination of doubt and hope churned his insides. He knew Getty was the creep who'd entered their bedroom twenty-nine years ago and taken his adopted sister. Hell, he'd been beating himself up about it his whole life, wondering why he wasn't taken instead. But now it all made sense. They were after her and only her. If he'd offered resistance, he'd be dead.

Getty and the man behind the mask had believed that Kimberly was a Beholder, and when they discovered her limited mental capacity, they left her wandering in the Quarter.

"There's a chance she's like Adelaide, Chief. That's why she was taken as a child, and I think she can help us now."

A shudder found its way across his skin as he reached for the sketches, took them from Danbury's hand and slowly stood up. In two steps, he made the chair next to her and sat down.

"Hey, sis," he said, patting her arm to get her attention. "I need your help."

Kimberly tilted her head to the side and looked at Royce. "Okay."

"I don't want you to be scared. I'm right here, and I would never let anything happen to you."

She frowned, drawing her brows together. "Okay."

"I want you to look at a picture and tell me if you remember the man in it."

She nodded and hunched her shoulders a couple of times.

Royce held out the sketch of Vincent Getty.

Kimberly pulled back. "Bad. He's a bad man."

Royce's pulse rate climbed, his senses shifting into overdrive. "Yes. He's a bad man, and he has someone I love. I want her back, but I need your help to catch him."

"Okay," she said, becoming more agitated with each passing minute.

"Did you see the man under this mask?" He held out the sketch of the Songe mask, with its gruesome features and distinct high ridge running from forehead to crown.

"He wants to hurt me, Royce."

"Did you see the man wearing this mask?"

She nodded, her eyes going wide as she began to rock herself in her chair.

"I need you to look at another man and tell me if you've seen him. Can you do that for me?"

"Yeah."

Royce looked up into Chief Danbury's face. "I need a computer with an Internet connection."

Danbury hurried out the door into the corridor and across to the nurses' station. Two minutes later he returned with an open laptop.

"Punch in this Web address." He rattled it off.

"Done."

"Now hit the biography section. There should be a picture of him."

"Here it is. Professor Charles Bessette, Cultural Anthropology." Danbury turned the laptop toward Beckett.

"Look at him, sis. Have you seen him? Was he the man who tried to hurt you?"

A low whine rumbled in Kimberly's throat and grew into a hoarse scream. She clapped her hands over her ears and closed her eyes, rocking so hard in her chair the legs lifted off the ground.

Royce waved Danbury back and gathered his sister in his arms. Stroking her head to calm her like he'd done to her as a child after the abduction, like he'd done after every terrifying nightmare Kimberly had, up until he'd sworn to catch the man responsible by becoming a cop.

"It's Professor Charles Bessette, Chief. He was one of Adelaide's professors at college. He drives a black diesel Mercedes. He and Getty are responsible for kidnapping Kimberly twenty-nine years ago because he believed she was like Adelaide.

"Maybe she is, maybe she isn't. The only thing that matters right now is he's got Adelaide, and I'm going after her."

SECOND CHANCES. Not many people got them, Royce knew as they rolled toward Bayou Gaudin and Bessette's ten acres of swampland beset with cypress, Tupelo gum and every slimy native creature born to the bayou. Hard to imagine Adelaide somewhere amongst that.

The afternoon heat was sweltering, leaping off the asphalt in watery waves.

Thunder heads hung on the horizon, mean, dark and building on the warm ocean currents driving Tropical Storm Linda straight for them.

A search of Professor Bessette's home in New Orleans proper and his office on campus hadn't produced anything, save a hostile reaction from his secretary and her assurance that Professor Bessette was on sabbatical.

The hell he was.

Royce knew it wasn't true, could feel it in his bones. Bessette planned to kill Adelaide tonight. Cut her throat and stuff her in the trunk of a car, just like her drawing had depicted.

Unless he stopped him.

Reaching up, he rubbed the torn gris-gris doll in his shirt pocket. His secret weapon against all of them, a weapon the professor had refused to touch the day they'd shown it to him in his office. An instrument of protection that had frightened Getty in the safe house.

But it was what he'd found inside the gris-gris that Adelaide needed to see.

The police radio broke squelch. "All units, go car-to-car scramble."

Royce pushed the scramble button on the radio, picked up the mic and keyed it. "Copy chief, unit thirty-four. I'm pulling off 90 West and heading due south along Rembrandt road. The turn into Bayou Gaudin should be marked. Bessette's property is situated between Gaudin and the main canal. There's a parking area two miles in on the left."

"Copy all units. Beckett is taking the lead."

Excitement mixed in his blood, tempered with caution. Bessette had been able to get away with murder for far too long. It was unlikely he'd surrender without a fight.

He slowed and took a hard right onto a narrow dirt road marked Bayou Gaudin on a crude wooden signed nailed to a cypress tree.

Sweeping nets of Spanish moss haloed the space overhead and darkened the afternoon light to eerie gray.

The road had certainly been traveled, judging by the deep ruts formed in dried mud that grabbed his tires and set him in the track.

It would be impassable if the rain hit.

"All units. This could be our location. Keep your eyes out for anything that moves. Getty said the ceremony would be at a grotto, so look for any type of shelter. A crypt is highly unlikely with the high water table out here, but we're dealing with a true believer, so anything's possible."

"Copy that, Beckett," Hicks said.

Royce put the mic down on the seat next to him and scanned the dense woods. It was impossible to see anything through the brush and foliage.

Bessette and his sect knew this bayou. Knew the canal and tributary system. That was how they'd placed victim number two, Wendy Davis. It was how the boatman had tried to escape with Adelaide.

Water.

Royce picked up the mic, his hand shaking as he keyed it. "All units, be advised, we're going to park our cars and head for the water, search along the tributary banks. I believe they may use the waterways to get in and out of here."

"Good call, Beckett," Danbury said over the radio. "I'll put the call out to the water rescue unit, have some officers in to patrol Bayou Gaudin and Main Canal. Up the odds."

"Copy that, Chief. All units rendezvous in the parking area at the tail of the main canal." Royce tried to settle his nerves as he made a left-hand turn off the road into a small clearing and parked the car.

He glanced at his watch. Dusk was just around the corner. He popped the trunk, got out of the car and went around to suit up.

In the distance thunder rumbled, setting him on edge. The storm was coming. They didn't have much time.

ADELAIDE LISTENED TO THE HUM of the motor, its vibration telegraphed against her cheek where she lay in the bottom of the aluminum boat.

She'd lost all track of time since being pulled from the trunk of the car. Behind the blindfold she tried to open her eyes, to get a look through a crack or a hole in the cloth, but it was pulled so tight, there was only darkness. Behind the tape, a bitter taste filled her mouth, and she sucked in several deep breaths to keep from gagging. Had she been drugged? It fit their sadistic MO, and the fact that she couldn't remember anything about the day.

Stretching out her bent knees, she made contact with something. It moved.

"Lie still," Vincent Getty said.

His gravelly voice made the hairs raise on her nape.

"We're almost there."

She could smell the pungent odor of swamp mud and decomposing plant matter. The bayou. But which one? The same one where they'd found Wendy Davis?

The boat slowed as Vincent must have let off the throttle.

The hull bumped and scraped along something. A dock, she guessed.

"What kept you? It's almost dusk. He's anxious to get started."

It was a voice she hadn't heard before. Maybe the driver of the car that hauled her away from the safe house. Away from Royce. Regret closed her throat, and she swallowed hard, working determination into her brain. She'd fight to survive. She'd fight to tell Danbury what they'd done.

"There were fishermen at the ramp. I had to wait until they pulled out before I could load her."

The boat tipped to the right. She felt it sway with Vincent's movements toward the bow to throw the tie line.

She rolled into the tilt, rocking the boat down hard.

"Damn!"

The boat jerked, then popped back to the left as Vincent fell out and hit the water. The splash showered her, and she prayed like crazy it brought the alligators. Hundreds of them.

"Get the boat." He came up sputtering. "Grab the line before it drifts away."

Someone else hit the water near the bow, and she felt the boat surge forward.

"Nice try," Vincent hissed. "For that I'll volunteer to dispose of you in Lake Cataouatche, after we slit your throat."

His threat ground over her nerves, but she'd become immune. She had nothing to lose fighting them every step of the way. She'd already lost what she wanted.

The boat pulled up onto the shore, hitting the bank with a thud.

The force lurched her forward. She smacked her head on something sharp. The bottom of the boat seat? Disoriented, she sat up, turned and felt for it.

If she could get a tear going on the tape binding her hands, she could free them.

Water churned next to her, displaced by heavy footsteps as someone trudged into the water beside the boat, and Vincent grumbled as he plowed out of the water on the other side of her.

Seconds ticked by like hours as she felt along the seat, found the sharp edge under it and raked her bound hands over it a couple of times.

Hands with an iron grip locked on her rib cage and she was dragged out of the boat, then dropped on the ground.

"Let's get her to the grotto. It's almost dusk," Vincent said from next to her.

Drops of water flew off him and dribbled on the top of her head.

Focus. Focus. She dug her thumbnail into the top of the duct tape where she'd scored it on the boat. It gave slightly and opened an eighth of an inch.

Above her on her right, she heard a knife snap open and lock in place with a decisive click.

Her heartbeat pounded in her eardrums and terror laced through her, but she continued to work the tear she'd opened in the tape.

"Cut her ankles free. I'm not going to carry her," Vincent said.

"Are you sure that's a good idea?"

"Do it. She's got nowhere to run."

She felt pressure on her ankles, felt the back-and-forth sawing action of the knife blade cutting through the duct tape.

He peeled it off, taking a layer of her bare skin with it.

Blood flowed freely back into her toes. She gritted her teeth against the sting.

A thick hand clamped on either side of her upper arms, and she was hauled up onto her feet.

The tape gave some more. She worked it with her fingernail.

"Is everyone here?"

"No."

They propelled her forward, and she did her best to put one foot blindly in front of the other as they walked over the soggy earth beneath her feet.

"Who's missing?"

"Derrick with the succinylcholine. He said the damn hospital was swarming with cops, said they turned it into a fortress when they brought a couple of their buddies in. He couldn't get into the drug room."

Vincent snorted.

Adelaide strained against the tape holding her prisoner. Could one of the officers in the hospital be Royce? Hope infused her as she worked the tape. It gave. She worked it harder.

"We'll have to do this the old-fashioned way. Ear to ear."

The man on her right chuckled. "I like it old school. It's a lot messier, but if it satisfies the cause, I'm all in."

She was halfway through the double wrap of tape.

Putting more tension on the tear, she felt it give for the last time and tear through. She held her wrists tightly together and prayed they hadn't felt the slack in her arms.

She had one shot. One chance to save herself.

Her toe caught in the earth, she stumbled forward, lost her footing and jerked against the pull of the men on either side.

Now. Adelaide planted her feet, heels down, and pushed back, catching them off guard.

"What the hell?" Vincent bellowed.

She pulled free, reached up and yanked the blindfold down. Light pierced her eyes, but she ducked to the side, just missing the swipe of Vincent's fist in her direction.

Adelaide bolted, staring at the path in front of her as she ran.

Boots pounded the ground directly behind her, and she reached up, jerked the tape off her mouth and sucked in a desperate breath.

Veering off the path she was sure led straight to the place they wanted her to be, she ran headlong into the brush.

Digging and clawing, she fought the pull of the undergrowth as it snagged her clothes and slowed her progress to a crawl.

Her muscles burned, her lungs expanding with each desperate gasp of air she pulled into them.

Branches splintered behind her.

Angry yells and grunts warned her of her impending capture, but she kept moving, kept hoping.

Then he grabbed a handful of her hair and yanked.

A scream tore from her throat, echoing and bouncing through the cypress, loud and desperate in her eardrums.

"I should kill you right here." Vincent's breath was hot against her ear as he reeled her in by her hair and locked his thick arm around her waist.

He dragged her back the way she'd come and planted her on the path. "Your mother was trouble, too. She managed to give me this." He brushed the deep, jagged scar on the right side of his mouth. "With a broken bottle, before I shut her down."

She held her breath and stared up at him.

Into cold black eyes that never blinked, never flickered.

"You killed her?"

"No. But I watched. She was planning to expose the entire sect. She had to die."

Adelaide lashed out at the thugs, kicking and scratching,

but they were stronger, and they easily captured her arms, stilling her resistance.

"Just like you killed Clay Franklin." She tried to catch her breath.

"He was a weasel. Staring in your window night after night. He's the one who told us about you after you drew the sketch of his mugger, but he couldn't get over his obsession with you. We couldn't risk the entire sect for one Peeping Tom."

"You were behind the wheel of the Mustang that night— you tried to run down Royce."

"Yeah. Too bad I missed your Protector when I had the chance, but he's done now."

A veil of hopelessness settled over her as they dragged her down the path, around the bend and into a clearing where a gaping hole opened in a dome built amongst the cypress using rock and earth.

There was death here. A feeling of finality she could smell on the rancid air, taste in the back of her throat.

Movement at the mouth of the crypt sent fear rushing through her as a man wearing the high-ridged Songe mask parted the curtain of Spanish moss and came toward her.

Her gaze traveled to the bowie knife in his right hand, to the way the fading light danced across the polished blade.

In silence he stopped in front of her and nodded his head.

"On your knees," Vincent ordered, pushing her down with pressure on her shoulder, until she sagged to the earth in a kneeling position.

Defiance claimed her heart and soul, and she spit on his shoes. "I'll never bow to you. You're nothing but a murdering SOB."

"Quiet," he bellowed, the mask distorting his voice, making it sound hollow.

He reached out and grabbed a handful of her hair, pulling and working it into a thick mass.

Adelaide trembled as reality knifed into her brain.

Humming deep in his throat, he jerked hard, raised the coil of hair and slipped the blade through it.

Adelaide gasped and rocked back, staring up at the madman who held a chunk of her hair in his hand.

"I've been waiting for you, Adelaide. Hunting for you from the time your mother took you and hid you before I could sacrifice you both. You look just like her."

"Who are you?" She wanted to understand. She wanted to know the truth, even if it killed her.

"You know who I am," he whispered. "I'm the man who killed your mother and you will join her. You will never be allowed to expose our acts of dark magic again. Bring her to the altar."

"Police. Drop the knife!"

Adelaide saw the man's arm come up at the same time she heard gunfire over her right shoulder.

The blade swung straight for her throat.

Another burst of gunfire, and she dived for the space between his legs.

The tip of the knife grazed the top of her head, and she went flat on her stomach, rolled over and watched the man in the Songe mask fall forward, a bloody hole in his back.

Several feet in front of him, Vincent Getty lay on the ground, next to the man who'd dragged her from the boat. Neither was moving. They were both dead.

She strained to see in the dim light as cops dressed in swamp-rat camouflage materialized out of the bushes and surrounded her. More of them rushed the flow of men wearing Songe masks as they poured out of the mouth of the crypt like spiders.

"Royce!" She climbed to her feet and glanced around,

recognizing Detective Hicks under a layer of bayou-green face paint and a reed-covered hat.

"I'm right here, babe." She turned and stared up into his face, focusing on his dark eyes in a sea of green.

"You didn't think I'd die and leave you all alone, unprotected, did you?"

She threw her arms around his neck and squeezed as hard as she could. Tears stung the backs of her eyes. She let them spill out and pulled in a breath before releasing him, but only a tiny bit.

Royce nodded to where the man in the Songe lay facedown in the dirt. "Hicks, let's get a confirmation on his identity."

Detective Hicks waved over Detective Lawton. Together they rolled the dead man over and pulled off the mask.

Hicks stood and shone his flashlight beam into Professor Bessette's face.

"Dear God," Adelaide whispered, staring at the man who had helped her to understand her gift.

"He killed her. He admitted it. The sketch was of my mother, not me."

Royce put his arm around her shoulders and pulled her close. "He's dead, Adelaide, you're safe, Kimberly's tormentor is dead and justice has been served." He pulled her away from the carnage and up the trail a bit, then he reached into the pocket of his fatigues and pulled out the headless gris-gris doll.

"I have something for you." He opened his palm.

"My gris-gris?"

"Look inside."

She took the doll and squeezed the neck opening, spotting the folds of a piece of paper hidden inside. A message from her mother from beyond the grave?

Blinking hard to see through her tears, she looked up at him.

"There's something I have to tell you first." She swallowed

"When I saw you dying on the floor of the safe house, I knew I loved you. And now that you're not dying, I still feel the same way."

He reached up and brushed her cheek with his hand. "When I saw the sketch of what we both thought was your death, at the time, I knew I had to protect you from it, and since you didn't die, I love you back."

Royce reached down, grasped her chin and tipped her face up so he could kiss her.

Deeply. Soundly. Forever.

Epilogue

Adelaide stared down at the paper in her hand and then back up at Royce, who sat across the desk from her in the hum of the detective division.

If she folded it one more time she was sure it would turn to pulp in her fingers, but she swore she could almost feel the desperation her mother had experienced as she'd secreted it away inside the gris-gris doll, knowing one day her daughter would discover it along with the truth.

What she hadn't been prepared for was the listing of her father's name on the document—David Laverue—and the subsequent information the revelation had produced. His thirty-three-year-old murder case, gone cold, now red-hot.

"Did Chester Mendoza make bail this morning?" she asked.

"Yeah, about an hour ago, and only because he gave us the details of the theft of adoption records from the Bureau of Vital Statistics, which Bessette used to track potential Beholders. We found Patricia Reed's information, along with Kimberly's. It looks like they were the only two he located with the records. Clay Franklin is the one who led Bessette to you. The other thugs we rounded up in the grotto have been charged with murder and denied bail, at least until we can determine what role each one played in the sect's crimes and the murders of the other non-Beholder women used in the ritual."

Adelaide pulled in a deep breath and leaned back in her chair. It had been two days since Royce had rescued her from certain death in the bayou, and with his help they'd pieced together a grueling tale of love and murder that reached well into the past.

"What are you going to do with the Songe mask once it's released to you from evidence?" Royce put his elbows on his desk and leaned closer.

"I think I'll donate it to a local museum."

"Not a chance, sweetheart. Your father didn't outbid Bessette at auction all those years ago so that the mask would wind up seeing the light of day. I think he purchased it so no one could ever exploit its dark magic. He bought it to protect your mother, and others like her. Too bad Bessette killed him to get it, and killed your mother to keep her from exposing him and his murderous sect. I say we honor your father's wishes in proxy and burn the hideous thing."

Royce was right. Any Beholder still out there wasn't safe as long as the mask existed, and there still might be someone willing to take up where Bessette had left off.

"You're right. I'll bring the matches if you bring the lighter fluid." She smiled across at him and slid her hand toward him.

He covered it with his and sobered. "On to other scary stuff. Are you ready to investigate the address written on the back of your birth certificate?"

She nodded, still clutching the faded document in her other hand. Closure was within reach. This was the last thing on her emotional to-do list, besides loving Royce and making a life with him. "I'm ready. Let's go."

ROYCE EASED THE CAR in next to the curb and turned off the engine.

Adelaide beat him out of the car and was standing on the sidewalk staring at the house as he joined her.

"This is the address. What are the odds anyone who knows her still lives here?"

"I don't know, Adelaide, but I can tell you no matter what you find here, I'll always love you."

Reaching out, she took his hand, then walked up the sidewalk to the front door of the little square house, painted a quiet shade of yellow.

She rang the bell and waited, trying to calm the spasms of tension in her stomach with a couple of deep breaths.

The door inched open a crack, then pulled open all the way, and she found herself face-to-face with an elderly woman.

"Yes. Can I help you?"

"Can you tell me if a woman named Sury Laverue ever lived here?" Adelaide's mouth went dry as she stared at the woman, studying her features for any resemblance to her own, and finding many.

"Yes. Thirty-three years ago, dear. I'm her mother, Virginia Wellington."

Adelaide felt her knees go weak and only the strength of Royce's arm locked around her waist kept her upright.

"I'm her daughter, Adelaide Charboneau."

The woman pushed open the screen door and stepped out onto the step. Reaching up with a trembling hand, she cupped Adelaide's cheek and smiled.

"Yes, you are, child. I've been praying you were alive somewhere out there, and here you are. Come in. I have so much to tell you about your parents."

* * * * *

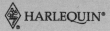

INTRIGUE

COMING NEXT MONTH

Available August 10, 2010

#1221 WANTED: BODYGUARD
Bodyguard of the Month
Carla Cassidy

#1222 COLBY VELOCITY
Colby Agency: Merger
Debra Webb

#1223 LOCK, STOCK AND SECRET BABY
Special Delivery Babies
Cassie Miles

#1224 ONE TOUGH MARINE
Cooper Justice
Paula Graves

#1225 ALPHA WARRIOR
Long Mountain Heroes
Aimée Thurlo

#1226 BUNDLE OF TROUBLE
Elle James

HICNM0710

LARGER-PRINT BOOKS!

GET 2 FREE LARGER-PRINT NOVELS

PLUS 2 FREE GIFTS!

HARLEQUIN®

INTRIGUE®

Breathtaking Romantic Suspense

HILP10R

HARLEQUIN®

A Romance

FOR EVERY MOOD™

Spotlight on

— Heart & Home —

Heartwarming romances
where love can happen
right when you least expect it.

See the next page to enjoy a sneak peek
from Harlequin® American Romance®,
a Heart and Home series.

*Five hunky Texas single fathers—five stories from
Cathy Gillen Thacker's* LONE STAR DADS *miniseries.
Here's an excerpt from the latest, THE MOMMY PROPOSAL
from Harlequin American Romance.*

"I hear you work miracles," Nate Hutchinson drawled. Brooke Mitchell had just stepped into his lavishly appointed office in downtown Fort Worth, Texas.

"Sometimes, I do." Brooke smiled and took the sexy financier's hand in hers, shook it briefly.

"Good." Nate looked her straight in the eye. "Because I'm in need of a home makeover—fast. The son of an old friend is coming to live with me."

She was still tingling from the feel of his warm palm. "Temporarily or permanently?"

"If all goes according to plan, I'll adopt Landry by summer's end."

Brooke had heard the founder of Nate Hutchinson Financial Services was eligible, wealthy and generous to a fault. She hadn't known he was in the market for a family, but she supposed she shouldn't be surprised. But Brooke had figured a man as successful and handsome as Nate would want one the old-fashioned way. *Not that this was any of her business…*

"So what's the child like?" she asked crisply, trying not to think how the marine-blue of Nate's dress shirt deepened the hue of his eyes.

"I don't know." Nate took a seat behind his massive antique mahogany desk. He relaxed against the smooth leather of the chair. "I've never met him."

"Yet you've invited this kid to live with you permanently?"

"It's complicated. But I'm sure it's going to be fine."

Obviously Nate Hutchinson knew as little about teenage

boys as he did about decorating. But that wasn't her problem. Finding a way to do the assignment without getting the least bit emotionally involved was.

Find out how a young boy brings Nate and Brooke together in THE MOMMY PROPOSAL, coming August 2010 from Harlequin American Romance.

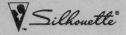

ROMANTIC
SUSPENSE

Sparked by Danger, Fueled by Passion.

SILHOUETTE ROMANTIC SUSPENSE BRINGS YOU
AN ALL-NEW COLTONS OF MONTANA STORY!

THE COLTONS
-OF MONTANA-

FBI agent Jake Pierson is determined to solve his case,
even if it means courting and using the daughter of a
murdered informant. Mary Walsh hates liars and,
now that Jake has fallen deeply in love, he is afraid
to tell her the truth. But the truth is not the only
thing out there to hurt Mary…

Be part of the romance and suspense in

Covert Agent's Virgin Affair

by

LINDA CONRAD

Available August 2010 where books are sold.

Visit Silhouette Books at www.eHarlequin.com

SRS27690

LOOK FOR THIS NEW AND INTRIGUING

BLACKPOOL MYSTERY

SERIES
LAUNCHING AUGUST 2010!

Follow a married couple, two amateur detectives who are keen to pursue clever killers who think they have gotten away with everything!

| Available August 2010 | Available November 2010 | Available February 2011 | Available May 2011 |

BASED ON THE BESTSELLING *RAVENHEARST* **GAME FROM BIG FISH GAMES!**

MCF810